She slid a pair of
heels from under
herself in. Witho
“You look hot.”

“Why, thank you.”

His instinctive response echoed through the big room. The only evidence she’d even heard him was the brief pause of her fingers at the last buckle before she slid her hands up her calves to swish her skirt back to the floor.

Was he flirting? Of course he was. Till that moment he’d never imagined the day he might wish he’d come back as a pair of shoes. But this woman was...something else. She was *riveting*.

“If I were you I’d lose the jacket, Mr Fitzgerald. It gets hot in here—hotter still once we get moving—and I don’t fancy having to catch you if you faint.”

Calling her bluff, he slid his jacket from his shoulders and laid it neatly over the back of the velvet chair. He tugged his loosened tie from his neck and tossed it the same way. Then he rid himself of his cufflinks and rolled his shirtsleeves to his elbows. Moves more fit for a bedroom than a dance hall.

Her gaze was so direct as she watched him losing layers it only added to that impression, and he felt himself break out in a sweat.

Then, with no apparent regret, she looked away, leaving him to breathe out long and slow. She pulled her hair off her face and into a low ponytail, lifted her chin, knocked her heels and Scheherazade was no more. In her place stood Dance Teacher.

Which was when Ryder remembered why he was there and *really* began to sweat.

Dear Reader

I am such a lover of dance movies I can't even tell you.

Singin' in the Rain, Strictly Ballroom, Girls Just Want to Have Fun, Footloose, Shall We Dance?... I've seen *Dirty Dancing* at the movies six times and a bazillion times since. And, boy, could I go on! But this is just going to end up being a list of the best dance movies ever if I don't contain myself.

So let's just say, despite all that fabulous training, it never occurred to me to write a story about dance. Then one day an image shimmied into my head—probably when I was in the shower, which is when all my best ideas spring forth.

Night—summer—sultry—sky on the edge of rain... And a man—tall, dark, smooth—in suit and tie, glowering up at a dilapidated building. This man is important, busy. He likes things neat and tidy and doesn't have time to waste. And yet there he is, about to head inside to take the first of what will no doubt be an interminable string of dancing lessons. Enter the dance teacher—exotic, hypnotic, raw where he is smooth, and as snarky as she is sensuous. I *sooo* wanted to see how that dance turned out!

If you love dance movies as much as I do I hope Ryder and Nadia's tale will take you somewhere familiar and new all at once. Then come and chat about your favourite dance stories with me on Twitter (*ally_blake*) and Facebook (*Ally Blake, Romance Author*), or e-mail me at ally@allyblake.com

Till then, happy reading (and dancing)!

Ally

www.allyblake.com

THE DANCE OFF

BY

ALLY BLAKE

Published in Great Britain 2014
by Mills & Boon, an imprint of Harlequin (UK) Limited,
Eton House, 18-24 Paradise Road, Richmond, Surrey, TW9 1SR

ISBN: 978 0 263 91077 3

Harlequin (UK) Limited's policy is to use papers that are natural, renewable and recyclable products and made from wood grown in sustainable forests. The logging and manufacturing processes conform to the legal environmental regulations of the country of origin.

Printed and bound in Spain
by Blackprint CPI, Barcelona

In her previous life Australian author **Ally Blake** was at times a cheerleader, a maths tutor, a dental assistant and a shop assistant. In this life she is a bestselling multi-award-winning novelist who has been published in over twenty languages, with more than two million books sold worldwide.

She married her gorgeous husband in Las Vegas—no Elvis in sight, although Tony Curtis did put in a special appearance—and now Ally and her family, including three rambunctious toddlers, share a property in the leafy western suburbs of Brisbane, with kookaburras, cockatoos, rainbow lorikeets and the occasional creepy-crawly. When not writing she makes coffees that never get drunk, eats too many M&Ms, attempts yoga, devours *The West Wing* reruns, reads every spare minute she can, and barracks ardently for the Collingwood Magpies footy team.

You can find out more at her website, www.allyblake.com

This and other titles by Ally Blake are available in eBook format from www.millsandboon.co.uk

For my Dom, whose snuggly hugs, gracious affability and eternal wonder makes my heart go pitter-pat each and every day.

Love you, baby boy.

CHAPTER ONE

LOOSE GRAVEL COURSING through the gutter slid and crackled beneath Ryder Fitzgerald's shoes as he slammed shut his car door.

Through the darkness of late night his narrowed eyes flickered over the uneven footpath, the barred windows of the abandoned ground-floor shopfronts, past big red doors in need of a lick of paint, up a mass of mottled red brick, over deadened windows of the second floor. The soft golden light in the row of big arched windows on the third floor was the only sign of life on the otherwise desolate street.

He glanced back at his car, its vintage curves gleaming in the wet night, the thoroughbred engine ticking comfortingly as it cooled. Since the closest street lamp was non-operational—tiny shards of broken glass pooled around its base, evidence that was no accident—only moonlight glinted off the black paint.

And he silently cursed his sister.

Glowering, Ryder pressed the remote to double-check the car alarm was set, then he glanced at the pink notepaper upon which Sam's happy scrawl gave up a business name and a street address, hoping he might have read the thing wrong. But no.

This run-down structure in one of the backstreets of Richmond housed the Amelia Brandt Dance Academy. Inside he would find the woman hired by his sister, Sam, to teach her wedding party to dance. And considering in two months' time he'd be the lucky man giving her away, apparently that included him.

A wedding, he thought, the concept lodging itself uncomfortably in the back of his throat. When he'd pointed out to Sam the number of times she'd done her daughterly duty in attending their own father's embarrassment of weddings, she'd just shoved the address into his palm.

"The instructor is awesome!" she'd gushed. *Better be*, he thought, considering the price of the lessons he was bankrolling. "You'll love her! If anyone can get you to dance like Patrick Swayze it's her!"

Ryder, who'd had no idea who Sam was talking about, had said, "Life-changing as that sounds, there's no way I can guarantee my attendance every Thursday at seven for the foreseeable future so you'll have to have your dance lessons without me."

Lucky for him, Sam had gleefully explained, the dance teacher had agreed to private lessons, any time that suited him. Of course she had. Sam had probably offered the doyenne enough to lash out on a six-month cruise.

"Your own fault she's so damned spoiled," he grumbled out loud.

A piece of newspaper picked up by a gust of hot summer wind fluttered dejectedly down the cracked grey footpath in response.

Ryder scrunched up the pink note and lobbed it into an overflowing garbage bin.

He tugged at his cufflinks as he sauntered up the front steps. It was a muggy night, oppressive in a way Melbourne rarely saw, and he was more than ready to be rid of his suit. It had been a long day. And the very last thing he wanted to do right now was cha-cha with some grand dame in pancake make-up, a tight bun and breathing heavily of the bottle of Crème de Menthe hidden in the record player.

But Sam was getting antsy. And he'd spent enough years keeping the *antsy* at bay to know revisiting the high-school waltz would be less complicated than dealing with one of his sister's frantic phone calls.

"One lesson," he said, wrenching open the heavy red door and stepping inside.

A Do Not Enter sign hung askew from the front of an old-fashioned lift with lattice casing. His eyes followed the cables to their origins, but all he saw were shadows, dust, and cobwebs so old they drifted lazily by way of a draught coming from somewhere it structurally ought not to.

Less impressed by the second, Ryder trudged up the steep narrow staircase that wound its way around the lift shaft, the space lit by a string of lamps with green-tinged glass so pocked and dust-riddled the weak glare made his eyes water.

And the heat only grew, thickened, pressing into him as he made his way up three floors—the ground floor apparently untenanted, the second floor wallpapered with ragged posters advertising student plays from years past. As it tended to do, the hottest air collected at the top where a faint light shone through the gap at the bottom of the door, and a small sign mirroring the one downstairs announced that the big black door with the gaudy gold hinges led into the Amelia Brandt Dance Academy.

Ryder turned the wooden knob, its mechanism soft with age. Stifling heat washed against his face as he stepped inside. He loosened his tie, popped the top button of his dress shirt and made a mental note to throttle Sam the very next moment he saw her.

The place appeared uninhabited but for the scent of something rustic and foreign, and the incongruously funky beat of some familiar R&B song complete with breathy sighs and French lyrics.

His eyes roved over the space—habitually calculating

floor space, ceiling height, concrete cubic metres, brick palettes, glazier costs. The tall wall of arched windows looking out over the street appeared to be original and mostly in working order—he only just stopped himself from heading that way to check his car was still in situ. From above industrial-size fans hung still. A string of old glass chandeliers poured pools of golden light into the arcs of silvery moonlight streaming across a scuffed wooden floor.

Speckled mirrors lined the near wall, and to his right, in front of ceiling-to-floor curtains that made his nose itch, reclined a sad-looking row of old school lockers with half the doors hanging open, a piano, a half-dozen hula hoops in a haphazard pile on the floor, a row of bookshelves filled with records and sheet music in piles so haphazard and high they seemed in imminent danger of toppling, and lastly a pink velvet lounge—the kind a woman would drape herself over in order to be painted by some lucky artist.

Ryder took another step, his weight bringing forth a groan from the creaky old floor.

The music shut off a moment before a feminine voice called from behind the curtains, "Mr Fitzgerald?"

He turned to the voice as his earlier prediction shimmered to dust. In place of a grand dame past her prime, Scheherazade strolled his way.

Long shaggy dark hair, even darker eyes rimmed in lashings of kohl, skin so pale it seemed to soak in the moonlight. A brown tank top knotted at her waist, showing off a glimpse of taut tummy. An ankle-length skirt made of a million earthen colours swayed hypnotically as she walked. Feet as bare as the day she was born.

Ryder straightened, squared his shoulders and said, "I take it you're the woman whose job it is to turn me into Patrick Swayze."

She blinked, a smile tugging briefly at one corner of

her lush mouth before disappearing as if it had never been. "Nadia Kent," she said, holding out a hand.

He took it. Finding it soft, warm, unexpectedly strong. And so strikingly pale he could make out veins beneath the surface. Warmth hummed through him, like an electrical current, from the point where their skin touched and then she slid from his grip and the sensation was gone as if it had never been.

"You're early," she said, her voice rich with accusation, and, if he wasn't wrong, shot with a faint American accent.

"A good thing, I would have thought, considering the late hour." He caught the spicy scent again, stronger this time, as she swayed past.

"And whose idea was that?"

Touché.

Light as a bird, she perched on the edge of the long pink chair, her dark hair tumbling over her shoulders in dishevelled waves, her exotic skirt settling about her in a slow sway. And Ryder wondered how a woman who looked as if she'd been born right out of the earth had ended up in a gloomy corner of the world such as this.

With a flick of the wrist, she hiked her skirt to her knee, revealing smooth calves wrapped in lean muscle. She slid a pair of beige shoes with small heels from under the couch and buckled herself in. And without looking up she said, "You look hot."

"Why, thank you." His instinctive response echoed through the big room. The only evidence she'd even heard him was the brief pause of her fingers at the last buckle before she slid her hands up her calves to swish the skirt back to the floor.

Was he flirting? Of course he was. The woman was… something else. She was *riveting*.

While she didn't even spare him a glance as she pressed herself to standing, poked a small remote into the waist of her skirt, and, shoes clacking on the floor, walked his way. "If I were you I'd lose the jacket, Mr Fitzgerald. It gets hot in here, hotter still once we get moving, and I don't fancy having to catch you if you faint."

He baulked at the thought, and for a split second thought he saw a flare of triumph in her eyes, before it was swallowed by the eyes so dark he struggled to make out their centres.

Calling her bluff, he slid his jacket from his shoulders, and, finding nowhere better, laid it neatly over the back of the velvet chair. Moth holes. Great. He tugged his loosened tie from his neck and tossed it the same way. Then rid himself of his cufflinks, and rolled his shirtsleeves to his elbows. Moves more fit for a bedroom than a dance hall. Her gaze was so direct as she watched him losing layers it only added to the impression.

Then with no apparent regret, she looked away, leaving him to breathe out long and slow. She pulled her hair off her face and into a low ponytail, lifted her chin, knocked her heels and Scheherazade was no more. In her place stood Dance Teacher.

Which was when Ryder remembered why he was there, and *really* began to sweat.

"Can we make this quick?" he said, recalling the reams of architectural plans curled up in the shelves by his bespoke drafting table at home. More awaited his attention inside the state-of-the-art computer programs back in his offices in the city. Projects of his and projects headed up by his team. Not that he had his father's trouble in settling on one thing; he simply liked to work. And he'd rather pull an all-nighter than spend the next hour entertaining this extravagance.

Nadia Kent's hands slid to her lean hips, the fingers at the top of her skirt dragging the fabric a mite lower. The faint American twang added a lilt to her voice as she said,

"You have somewhere else to be at ten o'clock on a Tuesday night, Mr Fitzgerald?"

"There are other things I could be doing, yes."

"So it's not that you're simply too chicken to take dance lessons."

His eyes narrowed, yet his smile grew. "What can I say? I'm a wanted man."

"I'll take your word for it. Now," she said, clapping her hands together in such a way that the sound echoed around the space and thundered back at them. "Where are your tights?"

"Excuse me?"

"Your dancing tights. Sam told you, I hope. If we are going to get any kind of indication of your aptitude you need to have the freedom of movement that tights allow."

He knew she was kidding. Okay, so he was ninety per cent sure. But that didn't stop hairs on his arms from standing on end. "Miss Kent, do I look like the kind of man who would have come within ten kilometres of this place if tights were required?"

He'd given her the invitation after all, yet when those sultry dark eyes gave him a slow once-over, pausing on the top button of his crisp white shirt, the high shine of his belt buckle, the precise crease of his suit trousers, his gut clenched right down low. Then her answer came by way of a smile that slid slowly onto a mouth that was wide, pink, soft, and as sensuous as the rest of her and the clench curled into a tight fist.

His voice hit low as he said, "If this is how you play with clients who are early, Miss Kent, I'd like to see how you treat those who are late."

"No," she said, "you wouldn't."

She slid the remote from her skirt, flicked it over her shoulder, and pressed. The sound of a piano tripped from hidden speakers, filling the lofty space; a husky feminine voice followed. “Now, Mr Fitzgerald, you’re paying premium to have me here tonight, so let’s give you your money’s worth.”

When she beckoned him with a finger, moving towards him all the same, saliva pooled beneath his tongue.

He held up both hands. “There is another option.”

There, he thought as a flash of anticipation fired in the depths of her eyes before she blinked and it was gone. But now he knew he wasn’t the only one sensing…awareness? Attraction? Definitely *something...*

“What do you say I pay you the full complement of lessons, and we call it a day? Sam needn’t ever have to know.”

“Great. Fine with me. But when you hit the dance floor on Sam’s wedding day, and all eyes are on you as you trip over Sam’s feet, what shall we tell her then?”

He wondered for a fanciful fleeting second if the woman might well be a witch. Less than five minutes and she’d struck him right in his Achilles’ heel.

“You done, Mr Fitzgerald? Because honestly, I teach two-year-olds who put up less of a fuss. You’re a big boy. You can do this.”

She lifted her arms into a graceful half-circle in front of her, an invitation for him to do the same. But when he did little more than twitch a muscle in his cheek, she swore—and rather colourfully—before she walked the final few paces, took his hands, and, with a strength that belied her lean frame, lifted them into a matching arc.

Up close he caught glints of auburn in her dark hair. A smattering of tiny freckles dusted the bridge of her nose.

Though his thoughts dried up as she fitted herself into the space between his arms and dropped his right hand to her hip. His palm found fabric, his fingers found skin. Smooth skin. Hot skin. Her skin.

She slid her right hand into his left and the heat of the night became trapped between them.

"Nadia."

"Yes, Ryder," she said, mirroring his serious tone.

"It's been a while for me."

The teeth that flashed within her smile were sharp enough to have his skin tighten all over.

"I'll go easy," she said. "I promise. You just have to trust me. Do you trust me, Ryder?"

"Not a bit."

The smile became a grin, and then her tongue swished slowly across the edge of her top teeth before she tucked it back away.

Maybe not a witch, but definitely a sadist, if how much she was enjoying this was anything to go by. "Nadia—"

"Oh, for heaven's sake! One last question. *One*. And then you shut up and dance."

Stunning, sadistic, and bossy to boot. An audacious combination. And, as it turned out, dead sexy. Which was why he made sure she was looking right at him, those eyes dark with frustration, before asking, "Who on earth is Patrick Swayze?"

At that she laughed, threw back her head and let rip. Her hips rocked against his, sending a wave of lust rolling through him. *Holy hell*.

Her hand landed firmly against his chest. "Let's not set the bar quite so high, hey, twinkle toes? My aim is to get you through three minutes of spinning on a parquet floor without embarrassing the bride." Curling her fingers slightly, she said, "Deal?"

While his blood thundered through his veins at her scent, her nearness, the press of her hips, her hand at his heart, Ryder's voice was rough as dry gravel as he uttered the fateful words, "Where do we start?"

"Where all great dance partnerships start: at the beginning."

As the music continued to swell through the huge room

she told him to listen to the beat. To sway with it. To let his hips guide him.

Gritting his teeth, he wished Sam had never been born. That helped for about five seconds before he gave himself a mental slug. While the kid might well be the one disruption in his otherwise structured life, she was also the best thing that had ever happened to him.

Eleven years old he'd been, only a few months beyond losing his own mother, when his father had remarried. A baby already on the way. Even as a kid, Ryder had understood what that meant—that Fitz hadn't been true to his mother; a woman with such strength, such heart, such insight. Worst of all she must have known it too, even as she'd been sick and dying.

When he felt the familiar sense of loathing rise like poison in his gut, Ryder shoved the memories back into the deep dark vault from which they'd bled. And instead hauled his mind to the day Sam was born. The first time he'd looked into his little sister's big grey eyes had changed everything. He'd vowed to never let her down, knowing already, even so young, that her father—*his* father—would disappoint, would deprive, would step over her to get ahead every chance he got.

And still, with that man as her paternal example, the sweet, clueless little kid was out there right now preparing to get married. *Married—*

"Concentrate!"

Ryder came to with a grimace as Nadia pinched the soft skin between his forefinger and thumb. He glared at her and she glared right on back. For a woman who felt like a wisp of air in his arms, she had strength to spare. "Honestly, Nadia, I don't need this. Show me how to get into and out of a Hollywood dip without pulling a muscle and we're done."

"First," she said, "it's Miss Nadia. Dance protocol. And secondly, the sooner you stop bitching and pay attention, the faster the time will go. Cross my heart." The scoop of her top tugged across her breasts as she crossed herself, the material dipping to expose the bones of her clavicle, the pale skin, the layer of perspiration covering the lot.

"Yes, Miss Nadia."

She liked that, clearly, breaking out in a soft laugh. "That wasn't so hard, was it?"

"You have no idea."

She might have brushed against him, or maybe he'd imagined it. Either way, hard was suddenly an understatement.

And as the hour wore on it didn't get any less so. Her hands seemed to be everywhere. Resting on his hips as she nudged them where she wanted them to go. Sliding slowly along his arms as she lifted them into the right position. Resting on his shoulders as she leant in behind him, pressing her knees into the backs of his to move his feet in time.

It was agony.

And not only because he wasn't used to being on the receiving end of such terse instructions. Though there was that too. Several years in charge of his own multimillion-dollar architectural firm, a guy got used to being in charge.

There was also the occasional waft of heady scent from that cascade of dark hair to contend with. The temptation of that sliver of tight skin above her skirt. And those *Arabian Nights* eyes tempting, beckoning, inviting him beyond the dance to places dark and sultry.

And then a knowing smile would shift across her lush mouth just before she counted loud and slow as if he were three damn years old.

When she finally turned off the music, he asked, "We're done?"

"For tonight."

Then, as if they hadn't just spent the better part of an

hour about as close as a man and a woman could be without their lowlier natures taking over, she simply walked away.

At the pink chair she pulled the band from her hair and shook it out, running her hands through it until it was a tumble of shaggy waves. As if she'd sensed him watching she looked over her shoulder as she bound herself in a wrap-around cardigan, and looped a long silver scarf around her neck. "Next time dress in loose pants, a T-shirt, and bring something warm for after. Even though it's crazy hot outside, your body will cool down dramatically after a workout like this."

Ryder didn't make any promises—he figured a fast cool-down was exactly what he needed. "I'll walk you down."

Her eyebrows disappeared beneath a wave of her hair. "Not necessary. I can handle myself. I'm a child of the mean streets."

Richmond was hardly mean, but, growing up with a little sister with a knack for climbing out of bedroom windows, Ryder had a protective instinct that was well honed. "It's eleven at night. I'm walking you down."

She gave him a level stare from those gypsy eyes of hers, then with a smile and a shrug she said, "A man's gotta do what a man's gotta do."

"There's that too."

He nabbed his jacket and tie and held them over his elbow rather than rugging up. She noticed, but said nothing, clearly considering herself off the clock.

She moved to an ancient bank of light switches and flipped the place into darkness, leaving only patches of cloud-shrouded moonlight teeming through the big arched windows, and Ryder's gaze was once again drawn to the soaring ceilings, the dusty chandeliers, the obnoxious industrial fans, and last but not least the fantastic criss-cross of exposed beams above, the kind people paid top dollar to reproduce.

Nadia cleared her throat and motioned him out, then with a yank of the door, a bump of the hip and a kick to the skirting board, locked up behind them.

He followed her down the stairs, the green glow of the old lights creating sickly shadows on the wallpaper peeling from the walls. But from topside looking down, the way the stairs curled around the shaft was actually great design. If the lift actually worked—

Irrelevant, he thought, with a flare of irritation. In fact the place should probably be condemned.

But Ryder didn't need a team of crack psychologists to tell him why the building continued to charm. It was just the kind of place his creative mother would have adored. Her legacy to the world was her wonderful sculptures made from things found, abandoned, forgotten, lost. Her legacy to her son was the knowledge that following your heart led only to heartache.

Pressing the memories far deeper, he redirected his gaze to the exit.

"Will I see you next week?" Nadia asked as they spilled out of the door.

"I fear you will," said Ryder as he turned on the cracked grey footpath to face her.

A step higher than he, she swayed sensually, hypnotically, from one foot to the other, as if moving to a rhythm only she could hear. Then she tipped up onto her toes bringing her face level with his. "Sam really has you wrapped around her little finger, doesn't she? I liked her before, but now I have a new-found respect for the woman."

Ryder sniffed out a laugh.

Then when she moved past him, jogging lightly down the stairs, he shoved his hands in his trouser pockets to keep himself from doing anything dangerous, like finding that slice of hot skin at her hips again and using it to drag her against him. Like losing his fingers in those crazy waves.

Like ravaging that smart, soft, tilting mouth till she stopped smiling at him as if she were one up on the scoreboard.

But Ryder held fast.

Because, delightful as she was, his only objective for the next few weeks was to survive until Sam's wedding without hiding her away in the top of a large tower where no man could hurt her. Getting all twisted up with the wilful and wily dance teacher, who he was fast gathering had become his sister's friend, would not help his cause one bit.

So instead of drowning in her dark eyes, her lush lips, all that dark sensuality so close within reach, he looked up at the building, past the big red door and up to the big sleeping windows on the third floor. "Do you know who owns this place?"

"Why?" she asked.

Because he was changing the subject.

"Something about the beams," he said, then glanced back to find Nadia halfway down the block.

"Don't ask me," she said over her shoulder. "I just work here."

Ryder watched her until she was swallowed by darkness, leaving him alone on the cracked pavement with his car, his skin cooling quickly in the night air.

Nadia fell into bed a few minutes before midnight. Literally. Standing at the end she let herself flop, fully clothed, face first onto the crumple of unmade sheets.

And the darkness behind her eyelids became a blank canvas as her memories began to play.

She could hear the creak of the stairs cutting through the song she'd been free-styling to. Could feel the disorientation of being caught out, leaving her breathless, sweaty, off kilter. Back on solid ground, wiping away the worst of her glow—*men sweat, women perspire, ladies glow,* her austere grandmother had always said—she'd peeked through the curtains.

Expecting a male version of Sam—tall, big grin, two left feet, handsome, sure, but slightly goofy with it—she'd been critically mistaken.

Ryder Fitzgerald was tall but that was where the similarities ended. Handsome had nothing on the guy—he was simply stunning. In that midnight suit, snowy white shirt, not a hair out of place, not a scuff on his beautiful shoes, he was big, dark, sleek, and razor-sharp. And to top it off, shimmering at the edges of all that relentless perfection was an aura of rough and raw sex appeal, as if the guy left behind an unapologetic testosterone wake.

When she'd ducked back behind the curtain her hands had been shaking. Shaking! Her breaths had shortened. Her stomach had curled tight and hot while her blood had thwacked against the walls of her veins. And all she had been able to think was, *Oh, no.*

With the grace of hindsight she could hardly blame herself. It had been over a year since she'd broken up with her ex after all. And if she was honest, longer again since she'd felt anything near that kind of all out, sweet, sinful, wonderful, carnal reaction to a man. For a woman whose entire life had been spent learning her body, knowing her body, celebrating her body, the fact that her body had become some sort of neutral zone had been damn near unnatural.

So much so, in her more wavery moments she'd wondered if something more than a two-year relationship had been damaged during the whole sordid mess. Even more than a bruised ego and a crumpled career.

But no, she was a Kent, and Kent women didn't cry over broken relationships—or broken bones for that matter. They got over it. Which she had admirably, thank you very much.

And then—right when she was doing so great, when she was dancing better than she had in her entire life, when she was mere weeks away from having the chance to reclaim all that she'd given up—right *then* was when the old flame had to flicker back to life?

Groaning, she rolled over and pulled a pillow tight over the thumping in her chest. It didn't help. Even with her eyes wide open she could still *feel* the play of muscle beneath the man's prosaic white shirt—hard, strong, a surprise. As had been his latent heat. All she'd had to do was touch him and she'd felt it pulsing beneath his skin. The exact same heat that had thudded incessantly through her for the entire hour straight.

Let it go, she thought. *The man's immaterial*. And heard her mother's voice.

Her mother who'd taken one look at Nadia when she'd turned up on her doorstep a year before with nothing but a suitcase and a sad story…and smiled. Not because she was glad to see her only child, oh, no. Claudia Kent's own ballet career had been ruined over a guy, and, seeing the product of that mistake in the same sorry position, she'd found herself looking down the blissful barrel of karmic payback.

Nadia gripped the pillow tighter, this time to stifle the woozy sensation in her belly.

Her mother might be completely devoid of any maternal genes, but at least Nadia had learnt early on how to cope with rejection, which for a jobbing hoofer was pure gold. One couldn't be precious and be a dancer. It was the tough and the damned. Ethel Barrymore had once said to be a success as an actress a woman had to have the face of Venus, the brains of Minerva, the grace of Terpsichore, the memory of Macaulay, the figure of Juno, and the hide of a rhinoceros. Working dancers needed all that *and* to be able to do the splits on cue.

Nadia had all that going for her and more. Yet if she didn't nail the fast-approaching chance to get her life back in a few weeks' time, she'd have deserved that contempt as she'd made the same mistake her mother did before her.

Well, not the *exact* same mistake—at least Nadia hadn't fallen pregnant.

With that wicked little kick of ascendancy fuelling her, she reached into her bedside table and found her notebook. For the next few minutes she pushed everything else from her mind and sketched out the moves she'd added to her routine that night before Ryder Fitzgerald had arrived.

In her early twenties she'd lived on natural talent, on chutzpah, and maybe even on her mother's name. A year out of the spotlight and that momentum was gone, and every day away younger, fitter, hungrier dancers were pouring into the void, eager and ready to take her spot. But what those hungry little dancers didn't know was that this time Nadia had an edge—she didn't simply want their jobs; this time she *really* had something to prove.

Sketches done, she slumped back to the bed. She'd shower in the morning. And since she didn't start work till two the next day, she'd have time to attend a couple of classes of her own—maybe a contemporary class in South Yarra, or trapeze in that converted warehouse in Notting Hill. Either way she'd kill it. Because look out, world, Nadia Kent was back, baby.

Despite the late hour, the last whispers of adrenalin still pulsed through her system, so she grabbed her TV remote and scrolled through the movies on her hard drive till she found what she was looking for.

The strains of *Be My Baby* buzzed from the dodgy speakers in her second-hand TV, and grainy black and white dancers writhed on the screen. When Patrick Swayze's name loomed in that sexy pink font, Nadia tucked herself under her covers and sighed.

Yep, things were still on track. So long as she didn't do anything stupid. *Again.*

Sliding into sleep, she couldn't be sure if it was her mother's voice she'd heard at the last, or her own.

CHAPTER TWO

"SO HOW WAS it? Was it amazing? Aren't you glad I made you go?"

Ryder pressed the phone harder to one ear to better hear Sam, and plugged a finger in his other ear to ward off the sounds of the construction site. "It was…" *Excruciating. Hot. A lesson in extreme—patience.* He tugged his hard hat lower over his forehead, and growled, "It was fine."

"Told you. And how cool is the studio? And the ceilings. I knew you'd love the ceilings."

No need to fudge the truth there. The beams were stunning. Old school. The exact kind of feature he'd once upon a time have sold his soul to study. He glanced about the modern web of metal spikes and cold concrete slabs around him, the foundations of what would in many months be a sleek, silver, skyscraping tower—as far from the slumped thick red-brick building as architecturally possible.

His foreman waved a torch in his direction, letting him know the group he was there to meet—and who were about to make his day go from long to interminable—had arrived. Ryder tilted his chin in acknowledgement, holding up his finger to say he'd be a minute.

"She was a dancer," Sam was saying. "A real one. A Sky High one."

Struggling to picture sultry Nadia Kent in a pink tutu and a bun, Ryder asked, "Nadia's a ballerina?"

A pause, then, "No-o-o. I told you. *Sky High*."

"Sam, just for a moment, treat me as if I am an Australian human male and speak plain English."

"Man, you need to get out more. Sky High is huge. A dance extravaganza. A kind of burlesque meets Burn the Floor meets Cirque du Soleil; all superb special effects and crazy-talented dancers. In Vegas!"

Ryder's focus converged until it was entirely on his sister's voice. "Sam, do you have a *showgirl* teaching your wedding party how to dance?"

"Oh, calm down. She wasn't working some dive bar off the strip."

And yet, picturing Nadia in fishnets, towering high heels and cleverly positioned peacock feathers wasn't difficult at all. Her pale skin glowing in the dim light, dishevelled waves trailing down her bare back, those lean calves kicking, twirling, hooking… Ryder closed his eyes and pressed his thumb into his temple.

"She's so graceful. And flexible," Sam continued, clearly oblivious to his internal struggle. "She was warming up the other night when we came in and she can pull her leg up so far behind her she can touch her nose!"

Ryder's eyes snapped open to search for a speedy exit from the conversation at hand. He had every intention of shrugging off the spark between them for Sam's sake, but the kid sure wasn't helping any.

Sam sighed down the line. "If I had half her talent, half her confidence, half her sex appeal—"

"Okay then," Ryder said, loud enough to turn heads. A few of his tradies laughed before getting back to nailing, laying pipe, measuring, chatting about the previous night's TV. "You like her. That's great. I'm taking lessons, as you wanted. Let's leave it there."

Sam might have missed his earlier silence, but he read

Sam's loud and clear. He swore beneath his breath as the hairs on the back of his neck sprang up in self-defence.

Sam's voice was an octave lower as she said, "She's single, you know."

"Got to go," Ryder growled. "My foreman's jabbing a finger at his watch so vigorously he's going to pull a muscle."

With that he rang off. And stared at his phone as if he couldn't for the life of him remember which pocket he kept it in.

There was no misreading what had just happened there. The kid was trying to set him up. That wasn't the way things were meant to go.

He was Sam's rock. Her cornerstone. Which was why he'd been so careful to keep his private life separate from his life with her; so she didn't go through life thinking all men were self-centred brutes like the father who'd failed them both.

Damn. Things were changing. Faster than he was keeping up. Faster than he liked.

For if he was Sam's cornerstone, she was his touchstone. His earth. As the raw ingenuity he'd inherited from his mother had been progressively engulfed by his own well-honed single-mindedness, and the crushing need to succeed that his father had roused in him, being there for Sam, no matter what, had been his saving grace. It had proven he was different from the old man in the way that mattered most.

Without Sam to look out for what would his measuring stick be?

To ground himself, he glanced up at the twenty-feet-high rock-and-dirt walls surrounding him, and imagined what would one day be a soaring tower; a work of art with clean lines, perfect symmetry, and a hint to the fantastical that pierced the Melbourne sky. It was the exact kind of project he'd spent more than a decade aiming towards.

Not that it had always been his aim to draw buildings that split the clouds. His first internship had been a fantastical summer spent in beachside Sorrento with a renovation specialist by the name of Tom Campbell, bringing the grand homes of the Peninsula back to their former glories. The gig had been hard, back-breaking labour, but the heady scents of reclaimed materials had also made him dream more of his mother, and her sculpting of lost things, than he had since he'd been a kid.

Until the day his father sauntered in with the owner of the home Campbell was working on at the time. Fitz couldn't even pretend it was accidental; the sneer was already on his face before he'd spied the hammer in Ryder's hand.

No ambition, he'd muttered to his friend, not bothering to say hello to the son he hadn't seen in two years. *Kid's always been a soft touch. Idealistic. Artistic mother, so what chance did I have?*

Damn those bloody beams for stirring this all up again. Because no matter how he'd come to it, the very different work Ryder did now was vital and important. And as for the woman who'd stirred other parts of him, hooking into his darker nature, begging it be allowed out to play? All elements of the same slippery path.

No. No matter how his life might be changing, his crusade had not. So he'd have to be more vigilant in harnessing his baser nature than ever.

With that firmly fixed at the front of his mind, he went off in search of the project manager, foreman, head engineer, the council rep, union rep, and the jolly band of clients, perversely hoping for a problem he could really sink his teeth into.

It was nearing the end of a long day—Tiny Tots lessons all morning, Seniors Acrobatics after lunch, Intermediate Salsa in the evening, so Nadia happily took the chance for a break.

She sat in the window seat of the dance studio, absent-mindedly running a heavy-duty hula hoop through her fingers. Rain sluiced down the window making the dark street below look prettier than usual, like something out of an old French film.

Unfortunately, the day's constant downpour hadn't taken the edge off the lingering heat. Nadia's clothes stuck to her skin, perspiration dripped down her back, and she could feel her hair curling at her neck.

And it wasn't doing much for her joints either. She stretched out her ankle, which had started giving her problems during her earlier weights training at the gym. It got the aches at times—when it was too hot, or too cold, or sometimes just because. As did her knees, her wrists, her hips. Not that it had ever stopped her. Her mother had famously been quoted as saying, "If a dancer doesn't go home limping she hasn't worked hard enough."

But it wasn't her body that had spun her out of the dance world. That would have been way more impressive, tragic even—a sparkling young dancer cut down before her time by a body pushed to the edge…

Looking back, she wished she'd handled things differently. That, after discovering her dance partner boyfriend had dumped her, hooked up with another dancer in the show and moved the girl into his apartment—leaving Nadia without an act, without a guy, and without a home all in one rough hit—she'd acted with grace and aplomb and simply gone on. Perhaps after kicking him where it hurt most. But whether it was embarrassment, or shock, or just plain mental and physical exhaustion, she'd fled.

The only *right* decision she'd made was in going straight to her mother. Oh, Claudia's gratification at finding her only kid tearful and dejected on her doorstep had been its usual version of total rubbish, but when her mother had told her to get over it and get back to work, it was *exactly* what Nadia had needed to hear.

Nadia went to work on the other ankle with a groan that was half pleasure, half pain. It meant she was dancing again. Meant she was getting closer to rekindling her life's dream.

But for now, she had one more class to go before she could ice up—her duet with Ryder Fitzgerald. She figured it was about fifty-fifty he'd show up at all.

And then, with a minute to spare, his curvaceous black car eased around the corner and into her rain-soaked view to pull to a neat stop a tidy foot from the gutter. Ryder stepped from the car, decked out once again in a debonair suit. *Nice*, she thought. He'd ignored her advice completely.

And then he looked up.

Nadia sank into the shadows. Dammit. Had she been quick enough? Last thing she needed was for Mr Testosterone to think she'd been waiting for him, all bated breath and trembling anticipation. She nudged forward an inch, then another, till through the rain-slicked window she saw he'd already disappeared inside.

With a sigh she slid from the window seat and padded over to the door. She twirled the hoop away and back, caught it in one finger and tossed it in the air before turning a simple pirouette and catching the ring on the way down.

She tossed it lazily onto the pile on the floor, plucked dance heels and a long black skirt from the back of the pink velvet chaise, and stepped into it so as to make the slinky black leotard and fishnet tights with the feet chopped off more befitting of the job ahead. Wouldn't want the guy to get the wrong idea.

Though if there was any man she'd met since coming home who she'd like to give the wrong idea… A week on and she could still remember exactly how good it had felt having the heavy weight of his hands on her hips. How lovely the strength in those arms, the hardness of his chest, the sure, slow, sardonic curl of his smile that made her lady parts wake up and sigh—

"Gak!" she said, shaking her head. Her hands. Stamping her feet. Anything to rid herself of the ominous cravings skittering through her veins. It didn't matter that she was a worshipper of the brilliance of the human body and all it could achieve *en pointe*, upside down, and most definitely horizontal; she'd be playing with fire if she went down that path. Her entire career hinged on what she did the next couple of months and that was not a gamble she was willing to take.

The beat of another set of stomping shoes syncopated against her own as the sound of a man's footsteps on the stairs echoed through the studio.

With a deep breath, she pulled herself upright, shoulders back, feet in first. She ran a quick hand over her ponytail, and then plastered an innocuous smile on her face as the door creaked open and the man of the hour stomped inside.

"Why if it isn't Mr Fitzgerald. I'd made a bet with myself you'd not show. Seems I won."

He glanced up, skin gleaming, wet hair the colour of night, the rain and heat having added a kink. A drop of rainwater slid from a dark curl on his forehead then slowly, sensuously down the length of his straight nose.

She swallowed before saying, "Get a tad wet, did we?"

He shook his hair like a wet dog, rainwater flying all over place. "This is Melbourne, for Pete's sake. It's tropical out there."

When Nadia was hit with a splat she called out, "Whoa, there! Ever tried dancing on a wet floor? Doable, but chances are high you'll come off second best."

She moved a ways around him, doing her all to avoid the puddles littering the floor, to grab a towel from the cupboard by the front door. Then turned and draped it from the crook of her finger.

His smile was wry as he realised he had to come and get it. Only he didn't look down as he took the three steps to take it, before rubbing the thing over his face and hair, all rough and random, in that way men did.

When he moved the towel to the back of his neck, eyes closed, muscles in his throat straining, Nadia gripped her hands together in front of her and pinched the soft skin at the base of her thumb to stop herself from moaning.

She must have made a noise anyway, as Ryder stopped rubbing and looked at her, hazel eyes dark over the white towel. Knowing eyes, hot and hard. Then he slowly, deliberately, held out the towel, meaning this time *she* had to go to him.

Eyebrow cocked, she barely got close enough to whip the thing out of his hand, only to be hit with a waft of his natural scent. Hot and spicy, it curled over Nadia's tongue until her mouth actually began to water. She dropped the towel to the ground and used her shoe to vigorously wipe the floor.

As if he knew exactly what was going on inside her head, Ryder laughed softly.

Nadia blamed the rain. Rain made people crazy. The last of the Tiny Tots that morning had literally gone wild, hanging from the barre like monkeys.

She hooked the towel over the heel of her shoe and flicked it up into her hands. "Now that's sorted, I think we need to take a step back."

"Back from where exactly?" he asked, his deep voice tripping luxuriously over her bare skin.

"Learn to stand before we start to move. Tonight we'll work on your posture."

"What's wrong with my posture?"

Not a single thing. "It's a process, Ryder. A journey we

are going on together. A journey in which I impart my wisdom and you do as you're told."

"So what are you telling me to do, exactly?"

She looked at him—hands in pockets, legs locked, suit jacket as good as a straightjacket for all the movement it offered him—and then, before she could stop herself, she said, "Strip."

Quick as a flash, he came back with "After you."

She hid her reaction—instant, hot, chemical—and, with a flick of her hand, she spun on her toes till she was standing side on. "Unlike you, I came wearing appropriate attire. Can you not see my spine, the equilibrium in my hips, the tension in my belly?"

So much for not playing with fire. The gleam in the guy's eyes turned so flinty it was amazing they hadn't sent up sparks.

Then, right when Nadia was on the brink of recanting her rash invitation, a muscle twitched in Ryder's jaw and his dark eyes began to rove. Over her neck, her collarbone, her breasts, her ribs, her belly, not lingering at any one spot longer than any other. Which only heightened the tension pulling at every place his eyes touched.

Point made—and points lost too, she rued—she slowly turned to face him, hands on hips as she waited till his gaze lifted to meet hers. "Take off your jacket, Mr Fitzgerald. And your tie. Dress shirt too, if you're game. You can leave on your singlet. I just need to figure out where your stiffness comes from."

He opened his mouth to say something, and then closed it. Instead merely leaving his gaze on hers as the double entendre remained, lingering on the air between them, all the hotter for not being touched.

Gaze snagged on hers, Ryder lifted his hands to his jacket, sliding it from his shoulders. Next came his tie. She had no idea where the things landed as she couldn't take her eyes from his. For then she'd have to look somewhere else. Somewhere lower.

But when his long brown fingers went to the buttons of his shirt, her disobedient eyes followed as he slid them through the neat holes of his perfect white button-down one by one.

He tugged his dress shirt from his suit trousers, slid it from his arms and laid it neatly over the chaise with the rest of his gear. As it turned out, the guy wasn't wearing a singlet after all. And when she looked up again, it was to find his eyes still on hers, daring, challenging, till defiance hummed between them, filling the dimly lit room so that the windows near vibrated.

"This what you were after?" he asked, the roping muscles of his long arms bunching as he held them out to the sides.

But Nadia couldn't answer; by that stage her mouth had gone bone dry. All she could do was nod, then busy herself with getting rid of the dirty towel. She somehow made it to the corner of the room and tossed it into the plastic bin. Curling her fingers around the edge a moment, she attempted to calm her thundering heart.

Okay, so asking him to strip had been a reflex action. The curse of a quick tongue. She was her mother's daughter after all. But she'd hardly thought he'd acquiesce. And how…

The men in her life had been lean. Not an ounce of fat on their undernourished bodies. Their faces on the edge of gaunt, the rest of them covered with the kind of muscle that clung in desperation to the bones. And waxed to within an inch of their lives.

Ryder Fitzgerald, with his hulking shoulders, big rolling muscles, thick thatches of hair beneath his underarms and whirls of dark curls all over his chest that dared not mar the taut, rolling muscles of his stomach before reforming in a flagrant V that disappeared beneath his trousers, might as well have been an entirely different species. Everything about him was bigger. Stronger. Lustier. Every inch of him gleamed with robust health.

And with one glance something primal had roared to life deep within her.

She glanced back over her shoulder to check if he was for real, and found he wasn't even watching her. While she was deep in the grips of a wave of impossible lust, hands on hips, back to her, he was staring up at the damn rafters!

"Right," she said, gathering her scattered wits and forcing herself to get a grip. "Clock's ticking. Let's do this thing."

Ryder turned; silvery moonlight and golden light of the old chandeliers pouring over him till his skin glowed, making the absolute most of the hills and valleys of his musculature. If the guy could actually dance he'd have given Patrick Swayze himself a run for his money.

With each clack of her heels on the old wooden floor, Nadia's tension ramped up and up. But this was a dance class. A close-hold dance class. Not touching him would only draw attention to her folly. At least that was what she told herself as her hand went to his shoulder.

His naked skin was silken, hot, it twitched at her touch, and the spark between them morphed into some living thing, twisting and shooting around them, filling the huge space with a crackling energy that struggled to be contained.

Nadia barely had time to take it all in, as Ryder didn't wait for instructions. He curled his fingers around her right hand, placed his other hand in the small of her back and moved deep into her personal space.

Her gaze was level with his collarbone, the scent of his skin so near she was lost within the mix of rain, heat and spice, her eyes so heavy she couldn't seem to lift them to his.

"Music?" he asked, his voice deep, low, intimate.

And it took half a second for Nadia to realise she'd yet to turn the damn CD player on. Snapped out of her haze, she swore under her breath and yanked the remote from the overturned waistline of her tights, and poked the thing in the direction of the stereo.

Norah Jones oozed from the speakers, warm and sultry. As she made to change it Ryder's hand came down over hers.

"Seems as good as any," he said, his gaze as good as saying, *Now you've got me where you want me, what are you going to do with me?*

What she wasn't going to do was tell the guy the song was too damn intimate for her liking, making her think of smoky jazz bars, and dark corners, and roving hands, and hot lips, and hot skin…

She lifted her chin, clamped her hand hard over his. "Start at your feet. Press them into the floor. Your leg muscles will switch on. Now soften your knees. Like you're about to bend them, without bending them. Press your inner thighs together—"

At that his hips pressed into hers and Nadia prayed for mercy.

"Lift your torso away from your hips, like there's a string coming out the top of your head and somebody's stretching you to the rafters. Now chin up, shoulder blades back and down and—"

"Breathe?" he asked, his voice strained.

The laughter that shot from her was unexpected, and he rewarded her with a small smile.

"Can only help."

Only when she felt in her bones, in that place inside her that knew dance better than it knew life itself, that they were positioned just so, she began to sway. Pressing his hand with hers, his thighs with hers, she tilted her hips to his until his movement matched hers. And even while every point of contact thrummed with awareness, dance-wise, compared to the week before, it was actually better.

"Feel that?" she asked several bars later.

"I feel something," he murmured.

"Not so stiff tonight," she said, and felt him turn to stone beneath her touch. "Oh, relax. I meant in the hips," she added, giving his arm a shake to get him moving again. "Been practising, have we?"

A muscle clenched in his jaw as he grumbled something about the better he knew the steps, the fewer lessons he'd have to endure.

"Really?" she said, honestly surprised. "Good for you."

He grunted. "I feel like I'm in one of those movies were you're about to ask if I could be your partner in some dancing contest."

She laughed again; this time it slid more readily through her. "Don't get ahead of yourself, sunshine. You couldn't keep up with me if you tried."

"No?" Without warning, he took her by the hand and twirled her out to the ends of his fingers. Years of training kicked in and she went with it, using her weight to hit the end and swing back where he swept her into a dip that left her breathless.

It wasn't the most graceful move she'd ever executed, and yet her breath thundered through her body as his dark shadow loomed over her, as his strong arm braced her back, as his striking eyes stared hard and deep into hers.

Her hands curled against his bare pecs, and for the first time she wondered about Mr Testosterone's life beyond the hour they spent together Tuesday nights. Did he lift cars for a living? Chop down hardwoods? No, not a bump in that perfect nose, not a single scar on that dauntingly flawless face…

Then, far more gently than she expected, he eased her back upright until they stood hip to hip, thigh to thigh, in a loose ballroom hold.

"How was that?" he asked, shifting so that she fitted closer still. Close enough to see flecks of gold in his hazel eyes. Close enough that every breath in was filled with his scent.

"Needs work."

"That's what I'm paying you for."

Well reminded, she pulled away and jabbed the remote until she found something less…Norah. A basic foxtrot, pure muzak, the least sexy sound on the planet.

"Your posture's closer," she said. "Now we'll work on your feet. Because, my friend, they suck."

Soon the hour was over. Sweat had added a sheen to Ryder's skin, a muskiness to his scent.

"Okay," she said, running her hands over her damp hair. "Work on your feet this week. Give me something else to pick on next time."

As she went to walk to the chaise to gather her stuff his hand clasped her wrist, stopping her. She looked back, hoping he couldn't feel the sudden flurry of her pulse.

"I thought it was something in the air, but it's you, isn't it?"

"I'm sorry?"

"That scent?" He leant into her, his nose brushing the edge of her hair as his eyes closed and he breathed her in. "I caught it last week too. Thought it was coming through the windows."

She opened her mouth to say…who knew what. Her throat locked up as her entire body stood stock still, riveted by the sensation of his intense attention, and all that intoxicating male body heat intermingling with her own.

"What scent might that be?" she finally managed, her words thick, as if she were speaking through a mouthful of marshmallows.

"It's spicy yet sweet. Like brandy."

She breathed in and figured it out. "Ah, my hairspray. Industrial strength."

His eyes moved to her hair, which was in its usual dishevelled array after a day's worth of dancing.

"I don't use it on my hair. Not unless I'm performing."

His eyebrows all but disappeared into his hairline. "Then where?"

"It keeps the leotard from rising."

"Rising?"

"Up," she said with a swish of her hand towards the offending area. And then she walked away, completely unable to help from looking back to find his eyes had zeroed in on her backside with enough intensity he might as well have been using X-ray vision to see beneath her skirt. And if she added a little extra va va voom to her walk? She was only human.

She grabbed her lucky black wrap cardigan, criss-crossing the cord around her ribs.

She turned everything off while her student made himself decent. Pity. It had been fun while it lasted. Heady, hazardous, but worth every agonising second. While it was imperative she keep her hands to herself outside the one hour a week, at least her fantasies now had something to live off for months to come.

As he had the week before, Ryder waited for her as she locked up, walking behind her as she headed down the rickety old staircase. It was kind of endearing, actually, or it would have been if the feel of him a step behind her didn't make her knees give out on the already precarious staircase.

When they got outside, he motioned to his slumbering car, all vintage curves and glossy gleam, its swanky dash glinting through the heavily tinted windows. "Can I drop you somewhere?"

She looped her big soft bag over one shoulder and gripped the strap in front of her. "Thanks, but no. I live just around the corner. And I'll be fine walking. I have a mean right hook." She lifted her hands in a boxing move, then backed away from the temptation of the cool luxury of the car, and the man who owned it.

His eyes remained steadfastly on hers. "Then would you like to get a coffee?"

Damn. Nadia nibbled her bottom lip and struggled to dampen the distinct tightening in her belly. "Thanks, but no. Hate the stuff. Stunts your growth, don't you know. See you next week."

Without another word, she turned and headed home, knowing he was watching as she walked away. She could feel it as surely as if his big hands were sliding down her back, over her backside, down her calves, deep into the arches of her sore feet.

Her pulse beat hard in her neck, her breaths coming tight and hard. And she was forced to ask herself, again, if she'd done the right thing saying no. A fling needn't be completely out of the question—

No, it needn't. Just not with Ryder.

The man had proven himself far too capable of wrong-footing her. And with the biggest audition of her life looming, she needed complete control of her feet. And the rest of her.

Yet, as she hit the corner, she looked back.

But Ryder was gone.

The heaviness that settled low in her belly had nothing to do with being alone in the dark. Living out half her teen years in New York, then Dallas, then Vegas meant it was nothing for her to walk through the shadows as easily as the pools of light.

No, it wasn't human company she craved; it was one very particular human.

She scuffed her shoe against a crack in the footpath and swore beneath her breath. Trouble lurked down that path, and, as was the fate of a Kent, she'd be the one who'd pay.

CHAPTER THREE

LIGHTS FLASHED THROUGH the darkness and music through speakers too old to handle the beat as bodies bumped and ground across the dance floor.

Nadia lifted her bare arms over her head, eyes closed, hips swaying, feet burning, as deep in her bliss she tripped the light fantastic. For her that was *exactly* how it felt; when the killer groove of the song met the rhythm in her bones, filling her muscles with liquid heat, and sparkling across her senses. It was approaching divine.

Add a fall of silk, a length of rope, better yet a sparkling silver hula hoop suspended thirty feet above the stage, adding danger, suspense, and an audience hushed with a mix of hope for a touch of magic and fear that something might go wrong… Now *that* was nothing short of orgasmic.

Feet well and truly on the ground—unless you counted three-inch spikes a prop—the vertical-drop strands of her fringed silver sparkly top swished over her belly, sensual, sexual, lifting the experience a nudge higher. Especially when she could so easily imagine the stroke of the strands belonged to the sure, sensual fingers of a man with dark hair and dark eyes and a dark voice that settled like a purr in her very core. Since she couldn't have him, she had to ease the sexual tension somehow, and dancing the hours away in a hip club deep within Prahran was the best way she knew how.

A sudden wave of dehydration swelled over her, condensing her vision to a pinprick. Knowing when she'd overdone it, Nadia wiped her hands over her face, slipped through the surge of sweaty bodies, and headed for the stairs that led down to the bar. And iced water. A jug of it for starters.

She skipped lightly down the stairs, doing a little twirl as the song upstairs hit its crescendo.

"Kiss me, Dancing Queen!"

Nadia felt herself grabbed. With a "Whoa!" she held onto a strong male arm, using momentum as much as the strength of his arm at her waist to haul herself upright. Then she looked up to find herself in the grip of a random guy. With golden curls and a wonky grin, he was cute as a button.

"What's in it for me?"

"My mates bet me a twenty you wouldn't. Too gorgeous, they said. Way out of my league. Do a guy a favour and show them different. I'll split it, fifty-fifty." The guy flashed his adorable dimple, proving no woman on the planet was out of his league.

When the dancing was as good as it got, it might even be better than sex, but sex sure had its place. And the guy was a serious honey. If she wanted a fling, a chance to scratch the itch that had been bothering her all week, this was it. Unfortunately the kick in her belly, the tension making her ache, wasn't his to erase.

"I'll have to pass." She grabbed his hand, ducked under his arm and twirled away, leaving behind a "Hey!" as she threaded through the lighter crowd to find the bar.

Instead she found that while she'd been dancing Sam and her friends had made their way downstairs too, taking up a group of soft velvet couches in a warm little alcove in the corner of the busy bar. Nadia walked that way in time with the smooth song crooning gently below the sweet murmur of conversation.

Sam stood and waved her over. Tall, skinny, knobbly; like a newborn colt. With her long straight dark hair and fey grey eyes Sam was quietly beautiful. Though, perhaps that was only compared with her brother's terrible masculine beauty, which was like a smack between the eyes.

Nadia nudged Sam's fiancé, Ben, to scoot over.

"Don't you go sweating on me, Miss Nadia," said Ben as he made space. "This jacket is suede."

Nadia eyed it, and raised an eyebrow. "That jacket is a travesty."

"See!" Sam called across the couch. She grinned past the straw between her teeth, the other end of which was deep in a tall glass of something poison green.

Nadia spied the jug of the stuff, mist wafting from the ice sprinkled across the top—at least she hoped it was mist—and poured herself a glass. Dancing hadn't erased the tight craving in her belly, and, since she'd stupidly given up a chance at a cute guy, poison-green cocktails might be her last resort.

She took a sip, shook her head at the beautiful bitterness, and settled into the lounge and the conversation swirling around her. The first real friends she'd made since moving home. Being able to talk about other things, fun things, silly things, serious things, things that had nothing to do with dance, was unexpectedly nice. Rare times she might even admit it was a relief. She'd miss them when she left.

Sam's eyes suddenly widened to comical proportions as she spied something over Nadia's shoulder. Enough that Nadia lifted herself from her slump and turned. And found herself looking into the hot hazel eyes of the man who'd sent her to drink.

"Ryder," she and Sam said at the same time.

Nadia clamped her teeth around the straw so as not to say anything else incriminating.

"The big man!" called Ben, pulling himself to half standing to extend a handshake to his future brother-in-law.

Ryder moved in to take Ben's hand, his shadow flowing over Nadia in the process.

He acknowledged the chorus of greetings with a smile in his eyes. Though when he finally looked down at Nadia, lifting his chin in acknowledgement, the glints hardened. Nadia crossed her legs to hold in the sensation that poured unbidden through her.

Belatedly, she noticed he'd changed. Gone was the ubiquitous pristine suit and in its place dark jeans and a dark sports coat. Beneath that an olive-green T-shirt that hugged the curves and definitions of his chest and made the very most of the flecks of green in his eyes. Nadia shoved the straw deeper in her mouth and took a hearty gulp.

"I'm so glad you came!" Sam called across the couch. "Was it the begging that did it? Or the promise of dancing? Ooh, you should dance with Nadia. Nothing like doing it for real to pick up some pointers."

Nadia bit down on her straw so hard her jaw hurt. Oh, Lordy, Sam was playing matchmaker. Nadia would have to put a stop to that. Meaning she'd probably have to explain why.

She'd managed not to tell a soul here her plans as yet. Not at the studio. Not her mother. And not Sam and her friends.

Not that she had any concerns of jinxing things. She'd never been superstitious though she knew many dancers who were: lucky shoes, miracle lipstick, turning three times on the spot while chanting "Isadora Duncan" over and over. It was a little more selfish than that—she'd moved on a lot in her life and knew how people began to pull away when a job was near the end. She wanted *this*—the ease, the acceptance—a little while longer.

"I just remembered!" Ben jumped in. "The Big Man's taking lessons too. I hear she told you you'd have to wear tights. Classic!"

Nadia opened her eyes wide at Ben but he just looked at her in sweet ignorance.

"Told you that, did she?" said Ryder.

"*She's* sitting right in front of you," Nadia muttered into her straw.

"How is he going, Nadia?" Sam asked. "I bet he tries to lead all the time."

Nadia smiled at Sam. "He's got potential, especially if he keeps applying himself."

"*Applying* himself to dance?" Sam repeated, eyes wide and suggestive as she grinned at her brother. "Well, I never."

Nadia made the mistake of looking up at the man in question to find his eyes glinting in warning. Unfortunately he didn't know her well enough to know that he'd just tossed fuel on her fire.

She blinked up at him. "Turns out he has excellent posture too. Quite the form."

Another beat went by in which the gleam in his eyes deepened, and the pulse in her wrist began to kick like a wild thing.

"In fact," she continued, evidently unstoppable, "I have a few amateur ballroom enthusiasts on my books who are desperate for a male partner. If I let slip about your brother here, there'll be blood in the water."

The muscle twitched in Ryder's jaw and he shoved his hands in the front pockets of his trousers, drawing her eyes down to what he'd framed all too nicely. Accident? Who knew? The man was an ocean of enigmas. Either way, by the time her eyes rose back to his, the pulse in her wrist had begun to beat loud and proud behind her ears.

Which was when the strains of a Kylie song filtered down the stairs and as one Sam's friends shot to their feet, babbling about the song and the school formal and somebody falling off the stage, before they were all gone up the stairs in the search of the dance floor.

Ben remained, stoic in his charge of the bags and chairs, and not about to get his new suede jacket anywhere near the sweaty dancers upstairs. Then with the couch all to himself he shuffled deeper, and spread out with a sigh.

"Want to get some air?" Ryder asked, not having moved an inch.

She looked back up at him, and up, and up. *Did she? Hell, yeah.* "You okay, Ben?"

"As a lark."

"Then air it is." Nadia put her cocktail back on the table and stood, running her damp hands down the thighs of her jeans.

She pointed the way to a balcony populated with beer drinkers and followed as Ryder made a way through the throng and to a quiet patch of railing. Music pulsed through the windows above. Soft chatter spread from the star-gazers outside. While Nadia breathed deep of the cool night air, the busy street below, the Prahran railway station peeking between the nearby buildings.

Then, without preface, Ryder asked, "When I asked you out for coffee, why didn't you tell me you had plans with Sam?" and with a darkness in his voice that Nadia hadn't seen coming.

Completely foxed by the direction of his conversation, her incredulity was ripe as she blurted, "Why? Do you have a problem with that?"

He stayed silent, but the twitch in his cheek gave her the answer.

"You do!" She jabbed his forearm with a finger; when it hit solid muscle it bounced right back. "What do you think

I'm going to do, corrupt her? Buddy, that venomous green potion masquerading as a drink back there was all hers."

Ryder's hands curled around the railing, the frown marring his forehead easing some. "She's…open-hearted. She's never been very good at protecting herself. That's long since fallen to me."

Okay, then. Not so much an indictment on her. This was about him. Nadia lowered her mental dukes. "I'd say Ben back there has you covered on that score."

Ryder scoffed, his frown back with a vengeance.

"What? Ben's smart, solid, and he's clearly smitten with her. I'm totally jealous."

"Jealous?" Well, that wiped the frown from his face. He turned to lean his elbows against the railing as he stared through the crowd at the young man scooched low in the soft seat, the collar of his jacket bunched up about his ears.

Nadia rolled her eyes. "Not of Sam, you goose. Of how much Ben adores her. I've never even been *close* to so adored."

Ryder's eyes slid back to hers, an eyebrow raised in raging disbelief.

"Admired by audiences, sure," she said, floating a *who cares* hand between them. "Envied by other dancers, oh yeah. Enjoyed by men, you can count on it. But adored?" She shook her head as Ryder continued to stare at her as if she'd grown an extra head. "Don't panic, Ryder. I'm not about to huddle in a corner and cry. A dancer's life is an endless series of rejections with just enough triumphs thrown in to keep us hungry. We're a tough breed, Kent women and dancers both. And it's hard to be tough and adorable at the same time."

"Puppies are adorable," said Ryder, his eyes now roving over her face, her hair, her shimmering silver top that she'd not all that long ago imagined slid over her skin with his touch. When his eyes roved back to hers she felt a good degree hotter. "Baby bunnies too."

"And your sister."

"Alas, my sister has a tendency to be that, to my constant disadvantage. As for you…" Nadia fought the urge to twist and turn under his heady gaze. "Adorable you may not be. But only because you're something else entirely."

The urge to ask what he thought was so acute she only just managed to swallow it down. If she went there, there'd be no going back.

Instead she leant on the railing and looked out into the night.

"My adorable sister is really marrying the twerp, isn't she?" Ryder asked at long last.

"Yeah," Nadia said on a relieved laugh. "Did you think it was all pretend?"

"No. Maybe." He ran a hand over his face, then through his hair, leaving it in spikes. And upon witnessing the first spark of vulnerability she'd ever seen in the man, Nadia felt her heart kick hard against her ribs.

In punishment, she bumped her hip against the railing hard enough to leave a bruise, and said, "I see what's going on here. It's like something out of a Jane Austen novel. The big sister—or in this case brother—overlooked, left on the shelf, while the younger sister shines."

As hoped, the ridiculousness smacked the vulnerability from his eyes. Then he grinned, his teeth flashing white in the moonlight. "Alas, I am a confirmed bachelor."

"Confirmed by whom?"

"Every woman I've ever been with."

Not dated. Not known. *Been with.* Nadia breathed deep.

"I'm a determined man when motivated, Miss Kent. And my motivations lead me to work eighty hours a week in a job I take seriously. I am less motivated to give up my standing holiday in Belize every Australian winter, one ticket return. Or full rights to the remote control. And at the end of the day I go home to the bachelor pad to end all bachelor pads."

"Posters of women in bikinis straddling large…motorbikes all over your walls?"

Guy didn't even blink. "No. But it's a damn fine idea."

"Yeeeahhh," she drawled, letting her grin out to play. "That's what I thought. And yet even with such a fine example of determined independence to steer her to rights, your sister has succumbed to the dark side. Give in, big brother. It's happened. Your little sister's all grown up. Time's nearing where you'll have to find someone else to boss around."

When Ryder stilled, Nadia wondered if she'd said something wrong. Pressed too far. But then his face creased into a rueful smile; his hazel eyes crinkled, attractive arcs bracketed his mouth, drawing attention to his fine lips.

Stern and formal, the man was breathtaking. Smiling, the guy could stop hearts.

Not quite able to catch her breath, Nadia turned away, enough to squint into the bar. Then, thankful she'd found a subject changer, she clicked her fingers. "I forgot to tell you earlier—I found out who owns the building."

He raised an eyebrow in query.

"It's in my bag, inside. Name and number. Remind me later. Or next week. If tonight's lesson didn't scare you off for good."

"First lesson I was asked to take off my jacket. The second you talked me out of my shirt. I couldn't possibly miss the third."

"Funny man."

"I try."

Nadia smiled. Then she shivered, realising belatedly how much the night air had cooled her down.

Without a word, Ryder shucked his jacket from his back and slid it over her shoulders. She curled herself into it, goose bumps springing up all over when she found it near scorching from the man's body heat.

"Ta," she said.

"Any time." And through the darkness he smiled.

Just like that something dislodged inside her.

It hadn't happened often in her life that someone had offered her much in the way of warmth, much less *any time*.

Her mum had left when she was two, she'd never known her father, and the grandmother who'd raised her could have played indifference for Australia. Looking back over the past months she'd come to see that her ex had treated her more like an enchanting sidekick than something necessary, something precious, and she'd stayed with him for two years.

Now some guy had given her a damn jacket, hardly the first time it had happened anywhere in the world, and yet Nadia held it tight about herself to keep ahold of the kindness as long as she possibly could.

Her voice sounded as if it were coming from miles away as she heard herself say, "Was it really just dumb luck that you and I both happened to end up here tonight, Ryder?"

Ryder watched her a moment, his dark eyes flicking between hers. Then he shook his head.

Her next breath in was shaky. "Sam told you I'd be here, didn't she?"

A nod that time.

"So you came to warn me off being her friend? Or was there another reason?"

Ryder swore, the word tearing from him as if he'd been holding it in all night. Then, without preamble, without waiting for permission, he slid his hand behind her neck and kissed her.

Light splintered behind Nadia's eyes at the touch of Ryder's mouth on hers, the sparks settling over her like a dream. She came out the other end, back to reality, to find herself melting. Her limbs liquid, her resistance stripped bare.

And Ryder fed her long, hot, wet, slow kisses. His fingers shifting through her hair, his body leaning slowly into hers.

She turned into him, sliding a hand over his shoulder, the other around his waist, over his backside, beneath the hem of his shirt till she found his scorching-hot skin. He groaned into her mouth. And she took it, opening herself to him, to his heat, his skill, his need that quickly ratcheted to meet her own.

“Ryder! Oh, sorry.”

Nadia heard the words, but Ryder pulled away long before she would have found it in her to stop.

“Sam,” he said, his voice gruff as it rumbled through Nadia’s bones. “What is it?”

“We were about to head off, and I was going to ask… Never mind.”

Nadia shook her hair from her face and lifted her head to look at her friend, who was steadfastly looking anywhere but at the two of them.

“Spit it out.”

“For a lift. But you’re busy. So I’ll get a cab. Don’t worry. Have fun and I’ll catch you later!”

“You going to Ben’s?”

“Well…no. Mine,” said Sam. “He has an early flight to Sydney for work, so I’m going home alone. He doesn’t trust me not to keep him up all night!”

At that Ryder turned to rock. “I’ll take you.”

And Nadia felt it like a loss. In direct proportional response, she instantly stepped away, ridding herself of his jacket, and holding it out on one finger, forcing Ryder to look her in the eyes. To apologise. Or at least look chagrined.

She felt as if she’d been winded when his eyes said something else entirely—he wanted her. Still. More. They weren't done here. And heat pooled in Nadia's belly with a ferocity even she didn't see coming.

"Take it," she said, her voice gravelly. "Give me five minutes upstairs again and I'll be hot to trot."

His eyes narrowed, and his mouth opened as if he was about to say something, something she would have paid a lot of money to hear, but, needing to steel herself against the sensations stampeding through her before they got the better of her, she threw the jacket at him, forcing him to break eye contact as he caught it.

Then he seemed to remember himself, and his sister, and with a nod he and his warm jacket and hot kisses walked away.

So sorry! Sam mouthed as she backed into the bar.

Nadia waved a "don't worry" hand, before shoving it in the back pocket of her jeans so she didn't have to see how much it shook. But Sam's third-wheel moment was the best thing that could have happened. Nadia'd been in danger of jumping into the guy's arms, wrapping her legs around him and not letting go.

When she could no longer see either Fitzgerald, Nadia made her way through the bar and to the bottom of the staircase.

She took one step up, the *doof doof doof* of the beat and the play of light at the top calling to her. But there she stopped, a finger pressed to her lips to find them swollen and tender. And she realised, for the first time in memory, she wouldn't find what she needed up there.

Instead, she turned on her heel and headed out into the night.

"So."

Ryder glanced in his rear-view mirror, changed down a gear as he neared a red light, and ignored Sam.

"You and Nadia, hey."

"Sam," he warned, when ignoring her seemed not to be working.

"Oh, come on. Anyone could see that you two have the hots for each other, even before I found you snogging on the patio." Sam shivered for good measure, while Ryder fought the urge to stick the car in Neutral and leap out of the door.

What the hell had he been thinking? He hadn't kissed a girl in a club in years. He knew privacy served a man better in that regard every time. And yet Nadia Kent slid under his skin and tapped right into his darkest instincts, making him forget all he knew. He ran a hand up the back of his neck and wondered how far things might have gone if they hadn't been interrupted. Till even the damn wondering made him ache.

"She is fabulous, though, don't you think?" asked Sam, settling deeper into the seat with a sigh.

Engaged though Sam might be, and clearly not the innocent little girl in plaits and frilly dresses she'd once been, he was not about to share with his twenty-four-year-old sister his thoughts on Nadia Kent.

Thankfully the light turned green, so Ryder could instead concentrate on grinding the gears and pressing his frustration into the accelerator. His car leapt from the starting gate with bravura and a gratifying press of backs to seats.

"And she's been brilliant for Ben and me," Sam continued regardless. "All this wedding stuff is stressful. We tried keeping it small but every time I look around it seems to have spread till I can't see to the end of it any more." Her voice trailed away with a soft sigh. "But as soon as we get to dance class it all just falls away. It's just Ben, and me. Nadia knows how to be unobtrusive, while at the same time setting the most romantic mood."

Nadia *unobtrusive*? Ryder couldn't think of a term that

described her less. Stick her in any room, and she'd be the most obvious thing in it.

"We call it Thursday Night Foreplay."

Ryder slammed on the brakes so hard the car shuddered beneath them. He eased off, caught traction and drove the rest of the way home five kilometres under the speed limit.

When Sam didn't say anything for a while, Ryder risked a glance sideways to find her smiling at him. Then she raised an eyebrow in question. With her big grey eyes and sweet face she might look as if she ought to be frolicking in a field of daisies, but she was his half-sister and had more than half his stubborn streak.

Gritting his teeth against an urge to tell her to mind her own damn business, he said, "She's your friend."

"So what? I'm a big girl. I can handle it. So don't let that be your excuse this time."

"This time?" he asked, then wished he'd kept his damn mouth shut.

Sam turned, gripping the seat belt. "You're eleven years older than me, man. You should be married with three kids by now! Don't think I don't know it's me who stopped you."

Ryder shuffled on his seat, never good at this part of it all. "Don't get yourself in a knot, kid. I don't do anything I don't want to do."

"Sure about that?"

Ryder's cheek twitched. Okay, so he'd been more circumspect than other men might have been. But he'd never seen it as a sacrifice. It had benefited him that the women in his life had taken his discretion as reticence for anything long term. A reticence that was entirely genuine, only for less altruistic reasons than Sam had put on him.

"I need you to know it's never been about you," he said, his voice steady.

"It's about Dad," she said with a bigger sigh. "You can't let him rule your life. You've told *me* so enough times."

He glanced at his sister then, and in her eyes saw prudence and wisdom. When had that happened? *Since Ben,* a little voice told him. Open-hearted she might be, but she was also twenty-four. He'd started his own company at twenty-four. "I own every decision I've ever made, Sam. Every one of them was ultimately all about me. About what I want my life to be."

She tilted her head towards him, the street lights flickering over her face. "Okay, then. And while we're on that subject..."

Ryder held his breath, sure Sam was about to hit him about Nadia again, and worried that in his wound-up state he wouldn't be able to convince her it didn't mean anything. Because that kiss had been...indescribable. Seconds, minutes? He had absolutely no idea how long it lasted, only that the micro-second he decided to go there his world went up in flames.

He felt himself unfold all over when she said, "Let's talk about me. I know that you've only ever wanted to protect me. To make sure I feel happy, and safe. And for that I love you more than you will ever know."

Ryder spared her a glance. "Right back at ya, kid."

"But I have Ben for that now. He's my knight-in-shining-armour, my prince, leaving you to finally just be my brother. Not my keeper, my minder, my shield." Sam put her hand on Ryder's on the steering wheel. "So in case you actually need to hear me say it, my big stubborn mountain of a brother, I hereby set you free."

The fact that she'd come to him for a ride an hour earlier seemed to contradict that, but when he looked at her he found she was serious.

"Free to date, to have lady friends—"

"Okay. Fine. I get it. I have your blessing to..."

"Shtup."

"For the love of..." he muttered as the gate to Sam's

apartment complex opened noisily at the press of a remote, before he rolled down the drive to the underground garage. "How about this—you and Ben can go right ahead and repopulate the planet all on your lonesome, so long as I don't have to hear about it."

She cocked her head, a frown marring her smooth forehead. "Ryder—"

"Didn't you just set me free?"

Her mouth twisted, then with a sigh and a nod she unhooked her seat belt, kissed his cheek, then leapt out of the door, and jogged to the lift. Ryder waited till she swiped the security card and was inside the lift up to her secure apartment before he turned the car around and headed for home.

By the time he threw his keys into a cut-glass bowl on the heavy table by the front door of his own split-level, waterfront residence it was well after midnight with more than half the working week ahead of him.

When restlessness began to flicker through him, he shook it off. He loved his job. It was extremely rewarding. Only at times, of late, he'd found himself wanting…more.

He glanced at the vintage drafting board in the corner. It had been his mother's. He'd been about three or four when she'd found it somewhere or other, cleaned it up, and placed it in a brightly lit corner of the family home. Over the years she would gravitate there to sketch out ideas. Ryder had drawn his first pictures of houses on that table, boxes with triangles for roofs. Multiple chimneys. Wings. Not tall buildings. Not back then.

He'd crammed the board into his bedroom after she'd died, and brought it with him to every place he'd lived since. He'd created the perfect corner for it when he'd built his own home—gorgeous down-lighting, a fantastic modern ergonomic chair, a wall of ten-foot-high shelves in which to keep old plans. And yet he'd never actually used the thing since she'd died.

Not about to change that, he ran his hands over his face and headed to his bar, where he poured himself a Scotch. Straight. He drank enough for it to burn its way down his throat, then sucked in a stream of cold air as a chaser.

His eyes glazed over the moonlit view of Brighton Beach and he thought of Sam's earnest face as she'd *set him free*, again struggling to picture what his life would look like without her as his responsibility any more.

But he had to ease off. To begin to let her go. She was ready. Or trying to be at least. *All grown up*, Nadia had said.

He emptied the glass, the burn not near strong enough second time around. At least, not enough to burn out thoughts of Nadia Kent. A woman who drew him in only to twirl out of his grasp. Infuriating. Intriguing. As for their attraction—it was wild, hot, barely in either of their control. It was like no other connection he'd ever felt.

But it didn't matter.

Sam was the reason he could look at himself in the mirror every morning and not cringe when he saw his father's jawline looking back at him. But even if the day came when she was no longer his number one focus, even with time on his hands and a hole in his life, he was not looking to fill it with a woman. Even one as enthralling as Nadia Kent.

He glanced again at his barren drafting table. Felt the restlessness rise, and struggled harder to press it down. Because the older he got, the harder he worked, the more successful he became, the less he was satisfied. And the more he wondered if, despite every effort to the contrary, he was beginning to experience the germination of his father's identical inability to endure. With work, with family, with relationships of any kind…

Ryder closed his eyes.

Of all his father had done in his life, it was the women the man had hurt who stuck deepest. His mother. Sam's mother. Hell, even when Fitz had been married to Sam's mother there had been so many others they'd long since morphed into a blur of false laughter and real tears. So many, even now Ryder found himself catching certain perfumes in a crowd and feeling nauseous.

In fact it was probably the smart move to remember. To shine a big bright light on their pain. Because he couldn't be sure he wasn't more like his father than he'd ever admit. Which was why he'd never risk committing to someone only to find out one day that it wasn't enough.

And even while he knew it was counterproductive, that he'd regret it in the morning, he purged the ugly memories as well as the cavernous blankness that was his future the only way he saw how.

Nadia.

He eased himself deep into an armchair, closed his eyes, breathed deep and found the scent he was looking for. Exotic, spicy, hot. Her taste erasing all others. The memory of her skin warming his ice-cold hand. The memory of her smart mouth easing the knot in his belly. Her red-blooded response to his touch, the burning pleasure, the aching tension, filling him up.

As he sank into every nuance of that kiss he wondered how hard the week would be, waiting to see her again. Wondered if he could. Wondered what it was about her that made him wonder at all.

CHAPTER FOUR

NADIA PACED, TRYING to diffuse the surfeit of energy coursing through her body, while out of the corner of her eye she watched the old clock on the wall as it ticked down the minutes to ten o'clock.

Rehearsing her audition piece hadn't taken the edge off; in fact her concentration was so shot she'd damn near killed herself! A friend had once broken a wrist rehearsing after a couple of champagnes. With the bumps and bruises now covering her body, Nadia was going to add Don't Fly Frustrated to the list of aerial acrobatic no-nos.

It had been a week since she'd seen Ryder. Since he'd kissed her till her bones had turned to syrup. And since then she'd spent every one of those nights writhing under the influence of the hottest sex dreams of her life.

Even the kids in her Tiny Tots class that morning had picked up on her dark mood, if the higher than average number of them clinging to their mothers' legs was anything to go by. Nadia had breathed deep and blamed the incessant heat of the past couple of weeks.

Sam hadn't helped either, making little comments through the entire lesson the Thursday before, laughing as she'd asked what Nadia's intentions towards her brother were.

Argh! She didn't need this. With her pedigree she could have taken her pick of classes populated with an embarrassment of hot young things with dancers' vigour, endurance, and sex drive, which was *why* she'd taken a job that put her in the path of senior citizens and two-year-olds in tutus.

Because she was *so* close. Less than two months now till the producers were coming to Australia. To see her. To give her a second chance. And she was ready. Pride mended, body more supple and stronger than it had ever been, ambition rekindled and honed to ferocity.

And then Ryder Fitzgerald had gone and kissed her and turned her into a walking livewire with the attention span of a fruit fly.

She was going to make him pay; it was the only way. She was going to work the man so hard before the end of the night he'd be begging for mercy. If he turned up, that was.

A minute ticked by. Nadia dragged her fingers through her shaggy hair before throwing her hands in the air and growling at the walls, her voice echoing in the lofty space.

"Should I come back later?"

Nadia spun to find Ryder standing in the doorway, the arch framing him like a painting. When her eyes rose to meet his it was to find his gaze was focused intently on her stomach, which was bare except for a silver Lycra bra-top over which she'd thrown a button-down shirt so she wouldn't cool down too fast.

Sensation feathered across her belly as she remembered all too clearly how those same eyes had looked the second before he'd kissed her senseless. All hot, and dark, and fierce. As if he'd wanted to eat her alive.

Frustrated to the point of pain, she wrapped the two sides of the shirt across her torso and near snarled as she said, "Honestly, would it kill you to take five minutes to change into something more comfortable?"

Just to make her feel more foolish, from behind his back he brought forth a gym bag. And it wasn't even new. It was pretty bruised and beat up in fact, with grass stains and sweat marks, as if the guy wasn't always immaculate, as if he knew how to get down and dirty if the situation called for it.

Nadia jerked her head towards the only bathroom at the far end of the hall. With a nod Ryder strolled away, one hand in his suit trouser pocket, pulling the fabric tight across his most excellent derriere.

Nadia whipped a couple of buttons through the holes of her shirt before yanking the tails into a tight knot above her belly button. She glanced at the clock. She couldn't even growl at him for being late. She'd find a reason soon enough.

She wouldn't be her mother's daughter if she didn't have a steel spine and a smart mouth. Both of which might have got them into trouble during their lives, but at least they always landed on their feet. Well, her mother had anyway; now retired and married to a mining magnate and living in an awful mansion in uber-posh Toorak.

Nadia, on the other hand, had spent her life climbing, reaching, happy to take her mother's scraps if it meant getting a lick of attention from the woman. But now all the climbing was done, and she was perched on the highest, thinnest branch, waiting for her moment to take the big leap into her own life. Nobody's scraps, no more. And nothing was going to stop her!

The far door creaked and she glared at Ryder as he walked her way, his suit now hung from a hanger in perfect straight lines. But as for the rest of him…

His feet were encased in battered trainers. Above them the calves of a runner, golden brown and covered in a smattering of dark hair. Knees lost beneath cut-off cobalt-blue track pants, the edges frayed from where they'd been hacked away. A long navy tank-top hung low and loose from shoulders gleaming with muscle.

Nadia swallowed right as her gaze hit his mouth,

meaning she didn't miss the moment it kicked into a knowing smile.

"Lose the shoes," she spat, turning and walking the hell away, ostensibly to find the remote for the stereo. "We're not playing hoops here, Ryder. This is dance class. Which means you need to be grounded. Connected to the music, to your partner, to the floor. And with the heat cooking this place tonight—" *and the mood she was in* "—you're gonna sweat more than you have in your entire life."

"Sweat I can handle."

"Yeah?" she threw over her shoulder. "Tell me so again in an hour."

His smile cocked higher, sending the pulse thudding through her straight to her belly.

He dumped the bag at the base of the chaise, hung his suit from a nail on the wall, and nudged his shoes off by their heels.

Oh, yeah, she thought with a secret smile of her own. A decade and a half of yoga had taught her the kind of pain that felt good when you were doing it, but kicked in with a screaming vengeance when your muscles came out of their trance thirty-six hours later. And he was going to feel each and every one.

That'd teach him to kiss and run. That'd teach him to mess with a Kent.

She pressed the requisite buttons. No more soft and swishy Norah Jones to make it easy on him. The hard thrash metal song chosen by a firm of accountants who'd hired her to choreograph a flash mob for their CFO's birthday thundered through the speakers, and for good measure she cranked it up.

As if the music wasn't making the building shake, Ryder ambled to their usual spot, near the centre of the room, beneath the soft glow of an ancient chandelier, and then held a hand to her.

As if that kiss had actually changed things. As if in giving her his jacket the other night he had shifted the balance of power his way.

Screw yoga, she thought, ignoring the temptation of that hand. Maybe she'd just stamp on his toes.

She was going to wipe that sexy smile off his sexy face, whatever it took. Because if the past few days proved anything, it was that if she didn't take control of this thing it would take control of her. And if she wasn't *completely* on her game come audition day, before she could say "Cyd Charisse" her reliability, her determination, her reputation as a serious dancer would be in question and any chance of a first-class professional dance career would be in ruins.

Nadia cranked the music up louder still, and, hands on hips, sauntered his way. Her eyes slid over him, as if she was trying to decide which part of him to hurt first as she worked him over and good.

Ryder stood stock still, his eyes on hers, until they weren't. They were on her hips. On her bare stomach. Sliding past her breasts. Before they landed on her mouth. And there they stayed, long enough the urge to lick her lips was overwhelming. When, despite herself, she gave in, he breathed in so long and slow his chest expanded till his top lifted, revealing a sliver of taut stomach, and a glimpse of the dark trail that disappeared into his shorts.

Nadia jabbed at the remote, shutting the music down. The silence that followed felt louder still. Stifling. Pressing in on her until she felt as if she were going to explode.

And explode she did. "Why on earth did you kiss me the other night?"

At that, the sexy smile finally disappeared, which gave Nadia about half a second's respite before Ryder's hot eyes cut right to hers. "Why do you think?"

"Argh!"

"Yeah," he said. "I figured by all the hand-wringing

that'd be about your answer. How about you answer me this: Why did you kiss me back?"

"I'm polite that way."

At that he laughed, the delicious deep sound reverberating about the room till it pelted against her skin like blissfully warm rain.

"You, Miss Nadia, don't have a polite bone in your body."

"I say please. I say thank you. If it's warranted."

"If you think it's not?"

"Then tough!"

His laughter this time was softer, deeper, more intimate. More knowing. It tripped and trickled all through her leaving a warm glow in its wake.

"Anyway," she said, shaking it off, "it doesn't matter why. All that matters is that we both agree, here and now, it won't happen again."

After the neat little speech he'd given her before the kiss, she fully expected him to agree. To make some excuse about how busy he was—eighty-hour weeks, solo winters in exotic Belize, the mysterious bachelor pad… About she and Sam being friends. How he was attracted to her, but…

"Why?" He took a step her way and, while her subconscious told her to bolt for high ground, she didn't move. "Why shouldn't it happen again?"

Simple enough question, with several fine answers. Yet as he prowled closer, all body heat and sex appeal, she could feel his wall of warmth before it should have been physically possible to do so, and there didn't seem to be a single reason why she shouldn't whip his top over his head and run her hands all over him, drag him to the floor and gain the release her body had been dying for all week.

At the very least she wouldn't send any more toddlers home in tears.

His hands gripped her waist, tugging her closer. She felt

her breath leave her in a whoosh. He smelled like man, and sex, and it had been so long it was all she could do not to whimper.

Instead, she found her strength in the only place it still resided—she lifted their arms into a dance hold. And breathed through her mouth so as not to be bombarded by his masculine scent.

When the song began, she pressed and he pulled. Then he stepped towards her a fraction before she'd been about to encourage him to do so, kicking her out of step. And again when the time came to turn, he moved ahead of the beat instead of waiting for her cue. The frustration gnawing at her from the inside out finally gave.

She ducked out from his hold and glared at him. "Maybe you're used to being in charge out there in those suits of yours, but in this room I'm the boss. Can you handle that?"

"I thought the man was supposed to lead."

"Only if he knows what the hell he's doing. Until then, it's my job to make sure you don't injure yourself."

"Somehow I get the feeling you'd like that very much."

"And there I was thinking how good I'd been at keeping my feelings to myself."

The words dried up as the two of them stared one another down, breaths coming hard and heavy, awareness licking between them.

A dark eyebrow kicked up Ryder's forehead. "Fastest way to a stomach ulcer."

His retort was so unexpected; Nadia coughed out a laugh. Then laughed some more. Laughed, a little hysterically actually, till she had to bend over and clutch her side. But, thankfully, a measure of the tension that had been coiling her in knots all week scattered along with it.

When she caught her breath she looked the guy dead in the eye. "Then this is how I see myself avoiding one." She counted off her fingers. "No more Hollywood dips.

No more flirting. No more pressing one another's buttons. And definitely no more kissing."

"I liked the kissing," he said, false contrition glinting in his gorgeous hazel eyes.

Yeah, she thought. *I hear that.*

Hands on hips, Nadia blew a wave of hair from her forehead. "Ever wish Sam hadn't decided on dance lessons?"

"Every damn day."

"Well, at least we're in step there." She checked the clock. Fifty minutes still to fill. "Speaking of Sam, she picked the song she wants the two of you to dance to. I think now's as good a time as any to hear it."

"Can't think of anything else I'd rather do."

A smile kicked at the corner of her mouth as she found the whimsical Norah Jones song Sam had chosen and pressed play.

Ryder's brow furrowed, before he nodded once. "I can handle that."

"Can you handle some choreography to go with it?"

Beneath his deep tan, the man paled.

"No pirouettes, I promise. Only one overhead lift, right at the end. It's tricky, but if you think you're not man enough to pull it off..."

His colour was back, and with it came a dangerous gleam in his eyes.

"You think I'm joking?" she asked.

"I think you have a sadistic streak. Makes me wonder why."

He said it as if it was a good thing, which sent utterly masochistic curls of pleasure straight to Nadia's belly. "I'm not a nice person."

"Nah, it's something else," he said, his gaze dropping to her mouth and staying there. "You're plenty nice."

"While you don't play fair."

"Where's the fun in that?" When his eyes lifted back

to hers they were lit with laughter. And heat. And promise. And absolute resolution. Despite her pleas he had no intention of backing down.

She looked at the impossible man before her in consternation. "You're really ready for this?"

"Raring."

You better be, she thought.

For the next half-hour she clapped out the counts as her old ballet teacher used to, till the shouts of her commands—*knees straight! shoulders back!*—echoed off the walls.

And soon they were both sweating. Not glowing, not perspiring, but dripping wet. While Sam's song trickled through the room like water over stones in a brook, looming rolls of thunder in the distance brought with them an oppressive heat the industrial fans above merely seemed to push about the room.

But Nadia didn't let up. Especially when Ryder actually seemed to respond. The man was tall and broad, which could make for a Frankenstein approach to dancing, but he had natural grace when he stopped trying to cage his instincts and just let go.

Nadia eased herself into Ryder's frame, adjusting only slightly, using her body to urge him where he needed to go. And this time, as one, their feet began to move. Slowly, gently, no push or pull, just the music pulsing through the floorboards and rocking them to and fro.

Nadia nodded. *Good boy.*

The music swelled around them, all harp chords and piano keys, and the singer's husky voice crooning about spinning round and round, moving so fast. Nadia moved Ryder forward, and then he moved her backward, the rhythm so natural she let him. He slid his hand an inch further around her back until her belly met his, and she let him do that too. He tucked their arms nearer their sides, which wasn't classic dance hold, but even while it made

Nadia's breath swell she didn't put a stop to it. The rhythm had other ideas as the dance swirled around and through them, binding them together and shutting out the world.

It was bound to happen, considering the way their bodies had fitted together in that kiss. That mind-blowing kiss—

Lightning lit up the room, followed by a crack of thunder, and then out went the lights. Then the fans. Music too. Not for the first time that week, but it was the first time they didn't flicker straight back on.

The heavy silence, the oppressive stillness in the air, the shards of moonlight the only thing between them, it should have been the perfect chance for Nadia to cut her losses and call the lesson over. Except neither of them stopped swaying.

In fact, Nadia might even have leant her head against Ryder's chest. Curled her fingers into the loops of his top. Melted a little when his chin landed gently atop her head. Melted a whole lot when his hands slid around her waist, across her tailbone, his thumbs dipping into the elastic of her skirt.

It was madness. Completely the opposite of what she'd set out to do with her hour. And not an altogether appropriate way to earn a fee.

But boy did she miss this. Not just the dancing, but the human connection. Skin on skin. Heat on heat. Feeling a part of something. Feeling discovered. Feeling *wanted.* And with every sway the sweetest sensation poured through her; a fragile serenity, not only filling nooks and crannies but opening them wide, till all that feeling pressed to the outer edges of her everything. And her heart became a bruising beat against her ribs.

Then, before she could talk herself out of it, she lifted onto her toes, wrapped her arms about Ryder's neck.

And then easy as you please her mouth met his. Hot, wet, open, lush.

His tongue met hers, and she turned to liquid, melting against him as if she wanted to vanish right on inside. And with a groan he lifted a hand to the back of her head, the other gripping her backside, leaving her in no doubt just how much he wanted this. And the warmth inside soon spun into a crazy heat.

She tugged his top over his head, all but growling at the sight of him. Rippling, hot, golden, even in shadow. No wonder she'd been so bent out of shape all week. How could she function on a normal level, when there was *this* to be had?

Her nails scraped through those tight curls of hair covering his chest and he sucked in a breath between his teeth, and grabbed her by the wrists.

She shot him a look through the darkness. *Really?*

And with a flicker of the muscle in his cheek, he eased his grip. Shuddering deliciously as she continued her exploration. All that heat. All that strength. She kissed her way across his chest, the salty taste of him turning her thoughts into a faint grey haze.

She felt him bunch beneath her touch before the groan tore from his mouth. And then his hands were on her shoulders, clever thumbs pulling her shirt away giving his mouth better access to her neck, his tongue tracing her collarbone, his teeth nipping the swell of her breasts. And when her collar slipped another inch and his mouth found her nipple, at the curl of his hot tongue she began to tremble.

Nadia dragged her fingers through his hair and held on tight as Ryder proved himself greedy, taking her mouth, taking everything he wanted, leaving her weak, loose, nothing but impulse, and sensation. With no thoughts to cling to except a dull buzz inside her head.

It buzzed again, and through the haze Nadia realised it was the trill of a phone chirruping through the heavy air.

When Ryder pulled away Nadia went with him, following his lips with hers. Not done yet. Not even close.

When she came up with nothing but air, her eyes flickered open to find his: dark, tortured. The want she saw there, the reckless desire, teetering on the very edge of control and chaos, scared her. Scared and *thrilled* her. Because it exactly mirrored her own.

But instead of throwing her to the floor and having his way with her, he said, "I have to get that."

That? Oh, the phone.

"It's nearly eleven at night," she said, her voice ragged, her fingers tugging at the beltline of his track pants. "You really don't."

"It's nearly eleven at night. I really do."

He unhooked her hands, gave them back to her, then turned his back and answered his phone. Leaving Nadia to wrap her arms about herself to control the suddenly very cold shivers wracking her.

Ryder murmured into the phone so that Nadia couldn't hear what he was saying. Then he hung up, and grabbed his things, turning to her only when he had everything in hand. "I have to go."

Nadia breathed out long and slow, slowing her heart, tempering the mortifying disbelief that this was happening *again* from ratcheting up to cyclonic levels inside her.

Then he dumped his things and swore effectively as he came to her, taking her by the arms and bending his head so that he was eye level, which was really the only reason she didn't boot him out of the flippin' door and demand he stay the hell away from her.

"Meet me," he said, command kindling at the edges of his voice. "Continue this. Tomorrow."

Not sticking a high heel in his ass was one thing, but asking for more? *Not on your sweet life, chump.* "I'm busy."

"All day?"

"Yep. Right this second, though? Not so much."

And there it was. If he wanted her, he could have her. Right there, right now. But not at his beck and call.

She'd been there, dancing to someone else's tune. And the fact that it wasn't a man who'd used her affections against her, who'd let her dangle, kept her at a distance even when they'd lived in the same city, danced in the same company, didn't mean it hadn't left a mean scar.

Ryder's jaw clenched, and he looked as if he wanted to shake her, or kiss her, or toss her over his shoulder and spank her. In the end he did none of the above; he rolled his eyes to the exposed beams he was so in love with, and left, muttering under his breath something about women being the death of him.

"Dammit!" Nadia cried out once he'd gone, shaking out her hands and pacing and kicking things.

If it wasn't so late she'd be on the phone to her boss telling her to find someone else to look after Ryder Bloody Fitzgerald. She'd absolutely do it in the morning. First thing. Before her feet even hit her cruddy apartment floor.

Till then…

Till then she stretched her arms high over her head, lifted till the arches of her feet screamed at her to stop, shook out her hair and danced to the sound of the rain drumming on the windows. Danced till sweat dripped into her eyes. Danced until her breaths grew ragged, her heart hammered, and her legs could barely hold her.

Power still out, muscles shaking and spent, she rugged up, turned things off as best she could, and left.

By the time she got downstairs, the storm had passed. And Ryder's luxe car was long gone. Not even a dry patch on the edge of the otherwise drenched and shiny street evidence he'd ever been there.

For that she had the burn of self-disgust riding deep in her belly and the crescents of still-tender love bites on her chest.

Nadia twisted her summer scarf into a ball at her neck, and walked the other way.

It was closer to dawn than midnight by the time Ryder turned onto the beach road leading to his Brighton home to find a pancake-flat, electric-blue sports car facing the wrong way and blocking his driveway.

Angry and frustrated, and wishing that he were back in his suit and not the ridiculous workout gear he'd worn to score points with Nadia, he pulled to a stop beside the outrageous car. The window of the mid-life-crisis-on-wheels slid down at a sulky pace.

Ryder said, "What do you want, Fitz?"

Ryder's father glanced up at Ryder's home, three stories of luxury living the younger Fitzgerald had designed himself, the daunting wall of dark windows looking out over Port Phillip Bay and the white stucco walls gleaming, even in the cloud-shadowed moonlight.

"Nothing more than I deserve," Fitz finally drawled.

Knowing he could spend a week giving his father the earful he truly deserved, considering the hour, and the fact that he wanted to spend as little time in the same vicinity as the man as humanly possible, Ryder decided on brevity. "I know what you tried to pull tonight. Just leave her the hell alone."

The man actually laughed, his light hazel eyes crinkling as he let loose a deep booming sound that made Ryder's teeth hurt. "Don't be ridiculous, kid. She's my daughter."

"And any *good* father would respect his daughter's decision."

"Respect? That's rich. Not only did she choose you to walk her down the aisle over me, she didn't even invite me to the damn wedding. I'm the only one should be harping on about a lack of respect right about now."

Yeah, Ryder thought, should have occurred to him "respecting others" wasn't a concept in his father's emotional vocabulary.

The man leant towards the window leaving only his eyes still in shadow. His infamous crooked smile, the one all those women had seemed hell bent on falling for, crinkled his age-defying face. "Come on, kid. Put in a good word. You know it's the right thing to do."

Ryder rolled his fingers into a fist before shoving it into the deep pocket of his track pants. Then he curled the fingers of the other hand over the window sill of the sports car, and felt a kick of satisfaction as his father reared back. "The right thing? Sam is your daughter, Fitz. One who has given you more chances to be an actual father than you could ever deserve. And your sweet, kind, only daughter is about to get married, and unlike you she plans for it to be the only time she does. So after a good deal of soul-searching she decided to spend that special day with Ben's family, a few close friends, her mother, and me. That's it. Because even while she loves you—heaven only knows why—she recognises that if you are there the whole day, her wedding day, will be about you."

Fitz scoffed, but Ryder went on, lifting fingers stiff from gripping the metal and pointing one at his father's nose. "And if you have even the slightest twinge of affection for Sam you'll do the right thing and suck it up. Because if you dare to turn up, if you send her a message, if you so much as *think* about her on that day…"

Before he did anything stupid, anything he'd truly regret, Ryder sucked in a deep breath and leant back, then he banged a fist on the roof of the car, only just stopping himself from denting it.

Either way, Fitz took the hint and with a kind of roar only a top of the range substitute for actual manhood could achieve he took off down the road in a screech of tyres and guttural noise.

Only after the sound of the car faded did Ryder close his eyes and suppress his anger. Or at least he tried. The man's influence echoed in the back of his mind, motivating him to do better, to achieve more, to prove the man wrong. But it had been a while, years in fact, since the effect had been so acute.

He couldn't remember feeling so incensed since that moment on the worksite during that long-ago internship, when his father had dismissed him so inexorably. A switch had flipped inside him that day. Emotions cooled. Ambitions honed. He'd lived that way ever since.

But in that moment he felt anything but cool. Standing on the quiet footpath, the first rays of morning blinking on the horizon, he struggled to get any hold of his emotions at all. His muscles screamed for relief. His heart pounded inside his chest.

And he knew that this time he didn't only have his father to blame.

He'd been playing with fire of late, in the hope he was cool enough not to get burned. Fire by the name of Nadia Kent.

The quixotic, bewitching, tempting creature had hooked herself into places deep inside him he'd long since kept locked away. She called to his darker emotions, luring them out of hiding. Feelings that could only do more harm than good.

And the whole time he was staring down his father, when his ire ought to have been *all* about standing up for Sam, there was no getting away from the fact that the deepest root of his fury was that he'd been dragged away from *her.* From that hellfire kiss that had been swarming them both headlong into something much more.

Not that he'd give his father an inch, ever, but the episode was just the wake-up call he needed.

With every effort he slowed his heart, reclaimed his breath, corralled the mixed emotions roiling inside him and pressed them back down. Deep. Deeper even than he ever had before, along with the big dark vault he kept especially for anything to do with his father.

Until the heat relented. His enmity abated. And every part of him felt blissfully, mercifully, icily cool.

CHAPTER FIVE

TIMES LIKE THIS Nadia wished she could drive.

Living out of hotels, or in share houses, there'd never been much point. But as her arms ached and her fingers turned numb under the strain of grocery bags she'd filled on her weekend trek to the Queen Vic Market it felt like a really long walk to the train.

And she wasn't even done yet.

The boom of boutique butchers competing for business thundered across the white noise of happy crowds while mounds of mouth-watering cheeses, curtains of speckled sausages, and trays of speckled brown, free-range eggs fought for greedy eyes. But the final stall on Nadia's list sold wine. Great, gleaming bottles of the stuff.

Nadia tipped up onto her toes and over the seething swarm of locals and tourists alike spied her target. Then, eye on the prize, she nudged her way through the crowd. When she stepped back to make way for a group of little old ladies sucking down fresh-made caramels she glanced away to discover that smack bang between her and the Promised Land stood Ryder Fitzgerald.

But before she had the chance to do anything about it Ryder looked up and straight into her eyes.

Surprise washed across his beautiful face. Surprise and heat. The kind that landed in the backs of her knees with a fiery *whumph*. But the moment passed as his brow furrowed into a scowl and wiped out everything in its path. *Seriously*, she thought, locking her wayward knees, like *he* had anything to damn well scowl about.

Resisting the desire to cut and run, Nadia stood stock still as Ryder began to stride her way.

She straightened her shoulders and lifted her chin. Not that it mattered any. She was dressed in her weekend gear of skinny jeans, pink ballet flats, a sleeveless top and thin summer scarf, her hair was a day late in the washing and twirled up into a messy bun, and she wore no make-up bar lip balm and wind burn. She was hardly at her best.

While he looked…breathtaking. His sharp jaw unshaven, his face all dark and glowering, his hair spiking up a little from the effects of the light drizzle outside, and in jeans and a dark grey T-shirt he was all broad shoulders and lean hips and the kind of swagger that came naturally or didn't come at all.

"Nadia," he said, her name in that deep voice doing things to her blood she had no hope of containing.

"Hiya!" said she in a high sing-song voice she'd never used in her life.

"Shopping?"

"Lunch. A bottle of wine to go with it, then home."

He eyed the two heavily laden bags then his eyebrows raised a smidge. "Expecting company?"

"Just me."

His eyes moved from her bags to her flat tummy, and she wondered if he could see the flutters she felt. Hoped not. Hoped so. Lost all hope in herself.

"Anyway, I need to get in line before it all sells out. So…" With a quick smile, she saw a gap in the crowd and slipped through.

She felt rather than saw him follow, the heat of the man burning against her back till she couldn't help but arch away from it. And then he was at her side, walking with her as if it was all planned. As if the last time she'd seen him he hadn't had his mouth on her, and his hands, and so very nearly more.

Knowing she couldn't outrun him, and needing that promised bottle of red more than ever, she said, "Doing a little shopping yourself this fine Saturday?"

He held up a bag of sugared almonds, before tossing one in his mouth. "Best in town."

Nadia tried not to stare as his tongue darted out to swipe the sugar dusting his lips, tried not to remember the other skills that mouth could boast without boasting at all. "They'd need to be if you braved this multitude for them."

A smile darted across his eyes, her tummy rolled over on itself, and she looked determinedly dead ahead. "So how's life been since you bolted Tuesday night?"

There, take that.

"Busy." The look he shot her was cryptic to say the least. Unfortunately it wasn't accompanied with anything like an explanation.

And that was as far as Nadia intended to go. "Ryder, I want you to know I asked my boss to assign your classes to someone else."

The guy actually looked surprised. His next step faltered, leaving him a beat behind. He covered it well though, as she expected he would. Blinded by all that simmering heat, it had taken her a while to see it; Ryder Fitzgerald was one cool customer. With a staggering ability to disengage himself, and his emotions, from one second to the next.

She'd known people in her life with that level of detachment. Had spent so long trying to get through that wall it had near crippled her. She could only be thankful she'd come out the other end. At least with the sense to know when to stick up for herself. And when to walk away.

Having reached the wine stall, Nadia lined up and kept her eyes dead ahead, but from the corner of her eye saw Ryder lean against the divider between the elevated stalls.

He said, "Am I to expect someone new to grumble over my feet on Tuesday night?"

"Turns out none of her other staff are stupid enough to agree to see a strange man at ten o'clock at night."

She shuffled forward a step.

"So it's still you and me?"

Nadia breathed out long and slow. Truth was she'd floated the idea with Amelia about shuffling Ryder's class to another teacher, but when Amelia had struggled to find a replacement she'd told her not to worry, despite the saga so far.

Kiss and run once, shame on him. Kiss and run twice, shame on her. There would *not* be a third time.

In a nice moment of helpful timing, she hit the front of the line before she could give Ryder his answer. Ignoring the man leaning moodily against the wall beside her, she chatted to her favourite stand owner—a dashing sommelier with the most charming French accent. The man was a total darling—in his eighties he could flirt with the best of them. Charming, innocent, simple. Oh that all men could be so.

Nadia bought her wine, and, still smiling, she turned to find Ryder watching her. There was nothing innocent, nothing simple about the way he looked over her with those dark eyes. From the muscle ticcing at his jaw to the bunched muscles of his crossed arms, he was a mass of coiled energy. And heaven help her if she didn't want to be right there with him when he uncoiled.

Wondering just how much she was going to regret it, she waited till his wandering eyes met hers, then said, "This isn't fun and games for me. It's my work. My life. I'll teach you on one condition. When we're in class I need you to behave and do as I say."

"Okay." Ryder didn't even hesitate. As if he really meant it.

Her success was short-lived as Ryder's eyes slid to her lips and stayed there, staring, glaring, as if he remembered exactly how she tasted and wished he could buy it by the ounce.

With a groan, she eased around the back of the queue and walked away.

"Where's your car?" he asked, on her heels again.

"I'm taking the train."

"Fair walk with those bags."

"Don't have a choice," she said, picking up her pace and shifting the weight of her bags. "I don't drive."

"Why on earth not?"

"I've lived in cities my whole life. Never needed to." Grimacing, Nadia went to shuffle the bags again, only to find herself relieved as Ryder reached out and slid them from her fingers.

"Thanks, but I can carry them."

Ryder glanced pointedly at her red hands, which curled into themselves in relief. He moved the bags easily to one hand, using the other to herd her, protect her from the crowd. "My turn to put in a proviso."

Of course. "What would that be?"

"That was rough, last week. I could barely bend over at work the next day."

Nadia let out a laugh, and when their eyes connected a gleam lit Ryder's eyes.

Nadia looked straight ahead. "And what kind of work would that be, needing for you to do so much bending over?"

"On a construction site."

"You're a builder?" Huh. "So what's with the slick suits, Ace?"

"Architect, actually," he said, the gleam morphing into a sexy smile, which, when surrounded by all that rough stubble, was as good as a loaded weapon.

"Is that why you're interested in my building, then?"

When he was silent a while she risked a glance to find his sexy smile had faltered. *Right, back to being Mr Tall Dark and Taciturn.* She gave herself a mental slap, and a reminder not to forget it. Not if she wanted to make it through the next month and a half without becoming unhinged.

"That's not the kind of architecture I do."

"What is?"

"High rises. Skyscrapers. Big, tall shiny ones."

"Ah, compensating."

His laughter came from nowhere, his eyes crinkling as deep waves of joy rolled from his lungs. People stopped. People turned. People sighed. People closed in as if magnetised. All of them women.

Rolling her eyes, Nadia shouldered past them out of the food hall and into the weak wet sunshine. "Your car's not that flash, though," she threw over her shoulder, in case he'd made it out of there alive, "which always gives a girl hope."

"My car is plenty flash," he said, having caught back up. "You've just never been inside her."

"Your car's a girl? My hopes for you are falling."

He shot her a look that was half lit with laughter, but mostly lit with something else. Something that made her feel as if baby ants were tap dancing all over her skin.

"So, Miss Nadia," he said, leaning in close enough his voice rumbled through her, "care to tell me about these hopes of yours?"

Her tummy rolled in honeyed pleasure. She bit her lip in atonement. "Not on your life, Ace. Now, why *not* bring back the glory of beautiful old buildings with beams strong enough to swing from if it's not about—" she glanced at his crotch and whistled "—you know?"

He blinked, then grinned. And the honeyed pleasure hardened so fast it fractured into a thousand pieces that pierced her insides with hot little spikes of desire.

"I interned with a few mobs after I graduated. The first commercial firm offered me a good package and I took it. Learnt a lot, learnt fast. Went out on my own a few years later."

"Hence the eighty-hour weeks."

"Hence. Helps that it's immensely satisfying work. For the most part..." The frown was back a moment before it slid away.

"Well, good for you. And I'm sure your...*towers* are awe-inspiring."

He shot her another of those glances, those new ones, filled with humour and that flicker of heat that he could never quite quell even when he was being all distant and haughty. This one came with a new angle, as if he was trying to figure her out.

"How about you—you like teaching?" he asked.

"It pays the bills."

"Damned by faint praise."

"Said the man who finds his own work satisfying *for the most part*?"

She expected a frown, and instead got a smile. The kind that slipped under her defences like a hot knife through butter.

Mmm. She'd need a flashlight, a map, and a millennium to figure *this* one out. She only had a few short weeks. Not enough time. Yet way too much.

She stopped and held out her hands for her bags. "Thanks for the help, Ryder, but I've got feeling back in my fingers. I can take it from here."

He just stood there, the muscles in his arms bunching as he slowly rearranged the bags, his dark eyes unreadable.

She clicked her fingers at him but he still didn't move. "Ryder—"

"It was Sam on the phone the other night," he said, the words seeming to tear from inside him. Then, "She was the reason I had to leave."

As if he'd thrown a bucket of warm water over her, Nadia felt herself pink all over. The heat grew when she remembered the one part she'd made herself forget—the torture in his eyes that he'd had to leave *her*.

Sam. Of course. But what didn't make sense was that he hadn't just said so. Unless…

Nadia swallowed, her voice barely above a whisper as she asked, "Oh, Ryder. Is she okay?"

He lifted an arm, as if to reassure her, then realised both hands were full. "Nothing like that. She's fine. But that night she was upset. Very upset."

Nadia kicked herself for not noticing anything at Sam and Ben's rehearsal Thursday night. It seemed the Fitzgerald family as a whole were good at keeping things close to the chest. "So what happened?"

"Our father happened," he said, and since he had her lunch and next day's leftovers in his hands, when he started to walk she had no choice but to follow.

"Your father's alive? I'd assumed… Since you're walking Sam down the aisle…"

Ryder's eyes became stormy. "He's well and truly alive, just not a part of our lives. He turned up at Sam's last Tuesday night. Tore strips off her for not asking him to walk her down the aisle. Father of the bride carries some social weight, don't you know. She was hiding out in the bathroom when she called; he refused to leave until she changed her mind."

While Ryder's voice grew hard as ice, Nadia's scalp

felt all hot and prickly as she tried to picture Sam huddled in her bathroom, scared of her own father. "Ryder, I'm so sorry. I had no idea. What a creep."

Ryder's mouth twisted into a wry smile. "No apology necessary. Though I'd go more for bully. Or asshole. Selfish bastard pretty much covers it as that comes with the knack for abusing the trust of anyone who dares care about him."

Ouch. Literally. Nadia's heart gave her such an unexpected little pinch she rubbed the heel of her palm over the spot.

"When she rang he was… I could hear him… While Sam was…"

He stopped. Breathed deep. While Nadia couldn't breathe at all.

"Sam's had panic attacks before, but not for a long time. Not this bad. She was so distraught by the time I got to her I ended up calling an ambulance. It was nearly three before she was calmed and back home asleep in bed."

Nadia's fist curled against her ribs. Poor Sam. Poor Ryder. While Nadia had been pouting and kicking things and generally thinking the guy was a big jerk, he was going through all that. She felt like a fool. Then, "Where was Ben?"

At that Ryder's granite gaze skewed back to hers. Behind the surface she saw such a deep river of concern it made her thumping heart twist.

"She didn't call him," said Ryder. "She only called me."

"Oh, no."

"Yeah. Pretty much my first thought too."

After a few loaded beats, they both began walking again, close enough they were as good as bumping shoulders. The ground was hot and steaming beneath their feet, the rest of the world a blur as they remained lost in their thoughts.

After a good minute, Nadia asked the one question that

had been left unanswered. "Where does your mother fit into the picture?"

A flare of something warmer pierced the granite. "My mother was…something else. A sculptor of found objects. A champion for the beauty redolent in bits and pieces others had cast aside. She could make something inspired out of detritus the rest of us wouldn't even notice." Then, as if he'd been working up to it, "She was sick for some time. I was eleven when she died. It took my father mere months to marry Sam's mother. And Sam was born weeks after that."

Nadia didn't ask how long after. She didn't need to. It was there in the set of his big shoulders, the tension of his beautiful mouth. His father hadn't waited for his ill wife to pass before knocking up wife number two.

Nadia couldn't imagine what it must have been like for a kid to go through that. Her relationship with her own mother was complicated, to say the least, but, even when she hadn't been around, she'd always been *there*. Even if "there" was the other side of the world.

In the end it hadn't taken a flashlight, a map, or a millennium. This big strong man had just given her a most unexpected glimpse behind the iron curtain. A glimpse at hidden depths, at the moral struggles that had been waged beneath that slick exterior. And even while she tried telling herself it didn't mean anything, that it didn't change anything, it felt like a precious gift.

Feeling a sudden urge to even out the score, Nadia picked the path of least resistance. "I never knew my dad."

Ryder's dark eyes flicked to hers.

"He was someone in the dance world, I gather. My mother was a dancer too. From bits and piece I gleaned over the years I think he was one of the owners of the ballet, or on the board." From the incessant mutterings of her sober grandmother, Nadia had also gleaned her mother had slept with the man in order to get ahead, and it had backfired spectacularly. No solos for a prima ballerina up the duff.

"Are you close to your mother?" Ryder asked.

"She lives in Toorak."

It wasn't what he'd meant, of course, and the clever glint in his eye, and hook to the side of his mouth, told her he was well aware of her prevarication. But he didn't push. Didn't ask for more than she was willing to give. This man holding her groceries. The same man who'd given her his jacket to keep her warm. The man who after every lesson—bar the one he'd fled to take care of his sister—had walked her out to make sure she stayed safe.

Emotions a little tender, a little raw, Nadia moved to the crossing lights, pressing the button to alert the machine she was there. When Ryder moved beside her, close enough now she could feel the shift of his body as he breathed, and goose bumps followed every time he breathed out.

"Hungry?" she said, before she'd even felt the words coming.

His gaze shot to hers, hot, dark, way too smart for his own good. Or hers.

But it was done now. Out there. The invitation for more. "Nothing fancy on the menu. Spare ribs and salad. Homemade cheesecake made in someone else's home. A bottle of really fine red."

He didn't answer straight away, and Nadia felt herself squirming in some deep, hot, hopeful place inside.

"I'm game," he said, his face creasing into the kind of smile that could down an army of women in one fell swoop. Then he started walking backwards, back towards the car park. "You cook, I'll drive. If you can bear to be taken about in my not so flash car."

She took a moment, as if mulling it over, all the while

her still raw and tender emotions indulged in the provocative smile that spread across his face.

Then she fell all too easily into step beside him.

Ryder sat on the opposite side of the wobbly kitchen table watching Nadia slide the last pork rib between her lips, her eyes shut as she sucked the last of the meat from the bone.

Either the woman had no idea he was pressing his feet hard enough into the cracked vinyl floor to leave dual dents so as not to make good on the urge to tip the table over and kiss that sweetness right from her lush mouth, or she knew exactly what she was doing to him and loved every second of it.

He figured it about a ninety-five per cent chance it was the latter.

In an effort to save himself from doing damage, Ryder took in his surroundings instead. Turned out her place was as much of a mystery as she was. He would have imagined lots of rich earthy colours and unusual bolts of light, perhaps even a secret passageway or two. Instead her apartment was small, neutral, and undecorated apart from the basics. In fact, apart from a few photos of dancers on the mantel over an incongruously blank wall, it was devoid of any personal touches at all.

And yet sitting in the shabby kitchenette of the tiny apartment above the abandoned Laundromat below, sunlight pouring through the grubby old windows, he felt himself relaxing for the first time in days.

And from nowhere it occurred to him that his colourful mother would have liked her. Would have been drawn to her spirit, her pluck, the way she seemed to fit in anywhere, yet not much care what anyone thought.

As for what he thought? From the first moment she'd walked towards him in the dance studio, all dark and mysterious and brazen, he'd thought her a creature of the night.

But in the bright, warm, quiet room he felt himself take that assumption apart and put it back together again.

In daylight her skin was beautiful, pale, and smooth. Threads of chestnut and auburn strung through her dark hair, which she'd twisted off her face showing off the most graceful neck he'd ever seen. With one bare foot tucked up onto her chair, her supple body curved over her food, she looked casual, content. And smaller somehow, softer without the va va voom and invisible whip that was such a part of her in teacher mode.

Which made it all the harder to remember why he'd spent the past few days carefully, determinedly distancing himself from thoughts of her. Disentangling himself from the desire that had wound itself around him like a straightjacket.

She licked her lips, and her eyes fluttered open. When she caught him watching her, she gave a husky laugh. The desire returned with all the force and ferocity of a rogue wave.

"Enjoying yourself?" he asked, his voice rough as rocks.

"Yes," she said on a long slow sigh. She flicked a glance towards the battered fridge-freezer in the corner of the room. "Dessert?"

He shook his head. Dessert wasn't close to what he wanted. "I'm not sure where you could fit dessert."

Her leg splayed to one side as she patted her flat belly and he had to hold back the groan that started right in his crotch.

Blinking innocently, she said, "Dancing is a damn fine workout, Ace. Which you'd know if you worked half as hard as I tell you to. I need all the energy I can get."

Ryder shifted on his seat, and struggled to find an innocuous change of subject so that he might get himself back under some semblance of control.

"Were you always a dancer?"

"Since the moment I came out of my mamma's womb," she said. "Family business."

Ryder stretched out the hand he'd bruised on the roof of his father's car and wondered at the kind of relationship where a child *wanted* to follow in a parent's footsteps. He nudged his chin towards the oldest photograph on the mantel—the image of a rake-thin dancer in full ballet regalia, her delicate face twisted in some tragic countenance. "That's her?"

"That was her. Before I was born. I've seen old videos," she qualified with a wry smile. "She danced like a whisper, soft, smooth, so quiet you'd never hear her land."

Nadia looked at the picture a little longer, blinked and sank her chin into her palm.

"Were you ever a ballerina too?"

She bolted upright at that, hand on her belly, mouth agape. "Good Lord, no! Do I look like a ballerina?"

What she looked was downright fit and lush and good enough to eat.

She let her stomach go, not that it went anywhere. "It takes a very particular kind of tenacity to make it in ballet, to have that level of control over your body. Over your whole life. Which is why Mum's ballet career was over the moment she fell pregnant with me. As for me, I like food too much."

Nadia waggled her eyebrows as she took a gulp of her wine.

Ryder quietly pieced together a relationship that might not have been so close after all. A mother and daughter living in the same city, yet not seemingly in touch. A mother who'd never revealed paternity. A mother who tangled the ending of her career and the birth of her daughter. And he shifted the conversation sideways.

"So if not ballet, what's your...speciality? Is that the right term?"

Nadia's mouth quirked and this time when she sank her chin onto her upturned palm the move was silken, slippery, sexy as hell. "I'm…well rounded."

"Learnt from Mum's mistake, then."

Nadia's laughter was scandalised. But she sank back into her chair with wicked wonder in her eyes. "I guess so. I've never been typecast, never been tied down to one style. I worked clubs in LA. A few stage shows in Dallas. My first solos were in a burlesque company off Broadway that was sold out for months."

Her gaze went to the mantel. Ryder's followed. "Seems a long way from ballet."

"You don't have to tell me. Especially considering Mum was working there at the time."

Ryder's eyebrows nudged up his forehead. "Well, I'll be."

While Nadia's eyes remained glued to the photo. "She'd always worked in America, but she had to leave her ballet company when she was pregnant with me and she came back to Melbourne. To my grandmother—picture Mum but humourless and grim."

Glancing at the photograph of Nadia's mother, Ryder thought it didn't take much picturing at all.

"Mum tried to stick it out once I was born. But when the dance calls…" Her fingers fluttered upwards in a move that seemed more of an impression than a natural movement of her own. "Then the life of a showgirl became too good to turn her back on. The hotel living. The rich men. The partying that reminded her she was still young, and helped her forget what she'd left behind…" Her eyes glazed for a second before she hauled herself back. "So I danced, and trained, worked my ass off and made it overseas. And then I got the call to work the burlesque club Mum had made her home. It was the first time we'd ever worked together, and I couldn't have cared if I was dancing Bollywood if it meant I was spending time with her. As for actually dancing with her?" She let go a long slow whistle. "It was amazing. For a little while. I was my own mother's protégé. We even had one act together, The Kent Sisters."

Ryder raised an eyebrow. But Nadia just grinned.

"I know. Hilarious, right? But despite *that* it was everything I'd ever dreamed of being since I first stuck my hands in the air and did a twirl."

"Since you're here, as is she, I take it things didn't last."

Nadia's gaze swung back to him as if coming from a long way away. She leant forward and cradled the glass of wine with both hands. "I got my first solo."

"Ah."

The wine was gone in a gulp. "And that was when she made it clear every job I'd ever been offered had only been after a phone call from her. That my name, *her* name, was the only reason I was anything at all."

Her mouth kicked into a wry smile, but Ryder caught the flash of hurt behind it. The disappointment. The disenchantment. He recognised the moment when you realised the parent you looked up to your whole life turned out to be, oh, so flawed.

"Anyway," she said, shaking out the funk that had settled over her, "after a particularly punishing day, I secretly auditioned for Sky High—at the last second using my grandmother's maiden name—and lo and behold got a place. Within the week I'd moved to Vegas, to the first real job that I'd ever been sure I'd got on my own. Not only that, it changed my life. Like I'd been dancing in shoes a size too small all my life and never known it. I'd found my bliss."

She finished with a soft sigh, a wistful and faraway gaze in her eyes. Then she looked around, seemed to realise where she was—or more precisely where she wasn't.

Her laughter was glib as she said, "I'm sorry. What was the question again?"

"I think you answered it." And then some. "I have just one more question. About your mother actually."

A flash of warning licked behind her eyes.

"She still pole dancing today?"

Nadia's laugh burst from her with such suddenness, such vivacious luxury, she near fell off her chair. "Ryder, if you knew her, you'd know how funny—I mean how *far off the mark* that was. A big Aussie mining magnate saw her on stage not long after I left New York, swept her off her pointy-toed feet and took her back home with him. She's retired. This time I'm the one who came home in disgrace."

"Back up a step now, Miss Nadia. Now we're getting to the good stuff. What did you do to disgrace yourself? Rob a bank? Sell state secrets? Arabesque when you were meant to…anti-arabesque?"

Her lush mouth quirked into a sensuous smile, before her face scrunched up in what looked like embarrassment. This was turning out to be a day of revelations. "It's nothing nearly so dramatic or exciting."

He waved a hand for her to go on.

"I broke up with my boyfriend, quit my job, and fled."

And somehow the idea of a boyfriend, a man, being this close, closer, to her, ever, made Ryder's hackles rise more than the thought of her making off with an armoured car. "Poor boyfriend."

Her cheeks pinked even as she smiled that sexy, exuberant smile of hers. "Missing out on all this? You bet poor boyfriend. But you know what? In all honesty?"

His eyes roved over her, the beautiful bone structure, the sultry dark eyes, the sensual way she moved. "Hit me."

"I've spent the past year convinced I left because of a relationship that went embarrassingly south. But I've been dancing professionally without a break since I was sixteen. I wonder if it wasn't really a blessing in disguise, if my body told me this was my chance to get away from it all for a while so that it could recuperate. If my ego saw the chance to eke out some time to just grow up."

She shrugged and sat back in her chair, her nose buried in the empty wineglass in her hand.

While Ryder couldn't quite feel his centre on the chair any more.

Because somehow things had…shifted. As if in the daylight, in her unassuming little flat, the normality of it all, having an actual honest conversation, caught at him, raw and arresting. Here sat a beautiful woman, slightly broken, but rich with substance and grit. And with his feet no longer pressing into the cracked old floor, there was nothing stopping him from perusing what his instincts had long since been screaming for him to do.

"Nadia."

"Yes, Ryder."

"You look plenty grown up to me."

The faraway gaze came back into sharp focus and her mouth curled into a smile. "I can assure you I am. All the way grown up."

And in the way that mattered most to Ryder, she was. What you saw was what you got with Nadia Kent. And there'd never been any question that what he saw he wanted.

"You missed some sauce," he said, eyes honed in on her lush mouth.

Her tongue flicked out to swipe the corner of her mouth. "Better?"

Better than what? "Still there," he lied, then lifted himself from his chair and leant over the table.

Her eyes darkened. "Ryder Fitzgerald. Not two hours ago you promised to be a good boy."

"And inside the dance studio, I'm yours to do with as you please. But I never made any promises about my behaviour elsewhere. And you never asked me to."

With a flare in her eyes that told him all he needed to

know, Nadia hopped onto her knees on her chair, and bent forward, met him halfway. “Care to help?”

“Hell yeah,” he said, leaning the last inch to cover her mouth with his.

He knew she’d be warm, knew she knew what she was doing; what he didn’t expect was the complete shock of pleasure that knocked against his insides like a pinball gone rogue.

Her hand lifted to his cheek, her fingernails scraping his unshaven chin, and he had to grip the table edges to keep himself from taking them both down in a heap.

She pulled away, leant her forehead against his a moment, then lifted her head to look into his eyes, her irises swallowed by the pupils. “All fixed?”

He breathed in deep, out hard and said, “Not even close.”

With that, she was on the table, crawling across the thing as it shook beneath her, the plates and cutlery bouncing to the floor with a crash. If she didn’t care, neither did he.

He hauled her against him, light as a feather, sinewy and soft, every movement pure grace, pure sex. No sweet kisses, all voracious hunger.

She tasted of lemon and honey and contradiction and heat. And her hands were all over him. Tearing at his clothes till he was naked from the waist up. Running through his hair. Scraping down his back till he growled from the pure deep pleasure of her touch.

Fearless, she was, and with a mouth that drove him wild.

Pulsing with a craving he could barely contain, he whipped her top over her head, her tight belly twitching beneath his palms, then her small breasts perfect in his mouth. So sweet, so firm, so sensual. The power in her warm, supple body was killing him.

Mouths open, hungry, a hand at his neck, she dragged him down. As she arched into him her hands found his zip, freed him. She enclosed her palm around him and slid down the length till he had to brace his feet so hard into the floor he saw stars.

She freed him only to wriggle out of her jeans, her body shuffling against him. His blood rushed so hard through his veins he felt as if his very cells were reconstructing, like some damn werewolf at the full moon. Man, he wanted her, with a ferocity he couldn't remember ever feeling.

"Got something for the big guy?" she asked.

"Wallet," he managed, "back pocket."

With a sure hand she found his wallet, taking a moment to caress his backside while she was there. The woman was wholly corrupting, whisking him to the very brink of desperation.

Once she'd freed the square foil from within she tossed his wallet over her shoulder, flicked the condom packet between them, grinning, then tore the thing open with her teeth. Then, dark bottomless eyes on his, she sheathed him. Slowly. Torturously slowly. And thoroughly. *Wow.* Her fingers traced every inch, and then some.

Her hands moved around his thighs, tugged at a few hairs, sending shards of pleasure and pain through every nerve, then her legs wrapped around him, tight and strong.

He nudged her centre, her slick heat near sending him over the edge. Her eyes fluttered closed, her mouth sliding open on a sigh, her brow furrowing as if he wasn't the only one teetering all too close to the edge of eruption. And then with a gifted flick of her hips she enveloped him, deep and tight and gorgeous.

From there Ryder's vision collapsed till it was the size of the table, everything else a red blur. His ears rang with nothing but the thud of his blood, with her gasping breaths. The scent of her, the feel of her, the sensual glory of her filling him from the inside and spilling out of him with a release so intense it near bled him dry.

He came to from wherever he'd gone, and realised his

arm actually shook as it kept him from collapsing on top of her. He opened his eyes and his heart shook right along with it. The woman was an exotic mess. Her pale skin pink and shimmering with sweat, strands of her dark hair having fallen from her bun and spilling over the tabletop, her mouth open dragging in breath, her eyes dark pools of desire.

And he realised with mortification he'd been so far over the edge of need he had no idea if she'd been right there with him. "Did you…?"

"Not yet." And she clenched herself around him with a strength that made his head spin.

She kicked a leg over his shoulder and rocked, her eyes clenching shut, her mouth open wide as she took in short sharp gasps of air. He had the feeling she knew exactly what she was doing, that she could have got there without any help from him at all.

But that wasn't going to happen. Not on his watch.

Ryder swore and braced himself on two arms. He felt himself harden inside her, pressed deeper and smiled as her eyes flew open. Then, holding her leg in place, finding it flexible enough to handle the stretch, he slowly lowered himself to bury his face in her neck, drinking in the scent of her. Kissing his way down her neck, her fine collarbone. He traced her knee, ran his thumb down her inner thigh, found her centre right as his mouth found her breast.

He plunged deeper and she cried out, gripping the table with one white-knuckled hand. The other scraping down his back hard enough to hurt.

His tongue traced her nipple, desire knotting his insides. He swirled his tongue as he swirled his thumb, and felt her tremble, and fracture, and melt. Heat slid through him at her acquiescence, at her trust, wiping out all but instinct, pleasure, her.

And when she stilled, when her body contracted around him, as her body trembled and rose and lifted and hovered once more on the verge of collapse he plunged as deep as he dared, his own second release coming from so deep inside he roared till the building shook.

Spent, he collapsed on top of her, her hand sank into his hair, the other flopped over her eyes, and together they lay there until their breaths eased back to near normal.

She moved first, and insanely he felt himself twitch inside her. *Enough,* he urged himself. Any more and the rubber would be irrelevant.

He pulled himself free of her, and his body felt instantly bereft. How soon it was used to her shape, her scent, the feel of her wrapped tight around him. How soon it wanted all that and more. Not sure that his legs would carry him just yet, he perched on the edge of the table.

Distractedly, he noted that the floor was a mess: broken plates, a fork end up into a crack in the wood, sauce oozing under the cupboard. But he didn't have the energy to care.

It hadn't been sex as he'd known it—it had been survival of the fittest. And he wondered what it meant that they'd both lived to tell the tale.

Nadia pulled herself to sitting and leant against his back, laying a string of warm kisses along his shoulder blade. "Wow."

"You're welcome."

Her laughter tripped over his skin, then she slid from her table, stepped over the mess, till she was standing, naked, in front of him. Lean hips, beautiful thighs, small breasts with the most perfect pink nipples, a belly he wanted to rub his cheek against.

"Shower?" she asked. "Not much hot water I'm afraid, so we'd have to share."

A hair band between her teeth, she lifted her lean arms to retie her hair back into a chaotic bun and simply awaited his answer. Not an ounce of self-consciousness in the move.

Just a woman who knew herself, liked herself, enjoyed the pleasure her body brought her.

For a man who'd spent a lifetime striving, soaring, hitting every pinnacle he'd ever aimed towards yet never reaching that illusive plateau of fulfilment, her effortless self-satisfaction was soporific, sinking into his bones like a drug.

"Coming?" she asked, a kick to her lush mouth.

Ryder didn't answer; his voice would have been little more than a hoarse croak as it was. Instead he lifted her up, threw her over his shoulder, her raucous laughter bouncing off the walls.

Then with a kiss to her gorgeous backside Ryder said, "Point the way, woman."

She did, with a neatly pointed toe.

CHAPTER SIX

THE SUNDAY SUN shone upon the breezy St Kilda bistro. The chips were salty and hot, the drinks icy cold, and as Sam chatted away about how her wedding plans were coming along Nadia tried not to flinch every time Sam mentioned her brother's name.

It was less than twelve hours since the tryst in her apartment, and she could still feel Ryder in the ache of her muscles, smell him on her skin, see him every time she blinked her damn eyes.

"I tried to keep it small, you know," Sam continued. "But everything seems to be spinning further and further out of our control."

"It's your wedding day, Sam," said Nadia, shaking herself into the present. Though she wasn't sure how she could help; as a kid the only time she'd imagined herself in a white dress was if it was a tutu. "Let that bossy streak of yours run wild!"

"Yeah," said Sam, rolling her fey grey eyes before they faded flat, and Nadia had a feeling she knew why.

Nadia nudged Sam's foot with a toe. "Ryder filled me in some on what happened the other night. With your father."

"He did?" Sam managed to look both relieved and like a puppy remembering it had been kicked.

"Are you okay?"

"Most of the time. Nothing the right pills and some

darned expensive therapy don't keep in check." When Nadia merely stared back, Sam put both hands over hers. "Honestly, I'm fine. The other night was horrible. Just really mean and ugly. But it only made me sure that I've done the right thing in cutting him off. Which, of course, my more astute brother did millennia ago. And speaking of Ryder. *He* talked about Dad? Using actual words? That's… I'm… Wow."

Nadia shifted on her seat. "Ryder didn't tell you we'd talked?"

Another eye roll. "Of course not. The man treats me like I'm made of glass. Though I get why. I do. What with his mum dying when he was so young, and our dad being… well, our dad, Ryder holds on crazy tight to the things that matter to him."

Sam curled her hands back into her lap and sighed.

"Don't tell Ryder this, but the only reason I'm going with a big white wedding is to give him the chance to give me away. I'd be happy to marry my guy right here, right now. But Ryder's so unwavering in his effort to do right by me I thought nothing less than an official ceremony would give him permission to really let me go."

Nadia nodded, even while she was only listening with half an ear. A warning bell had begun to buzz pretty insistently about a minute back when Sam had said *Ryder holds on crazy tight to the things that matter to him*.

It wasn't as if *she* mattered to him, not in the way Sam meant. Even if it was natural for a proprietary feeling to come into play when you'd been naked with someone, when that someone had taken you to heaven and back on your kitchen table, in your shower, and slow, tender, deep, trembling, and weak up against the front door, they'd never talked about the chance of an extended run. Or even going for a second act. In fact once their clothes had come off they'd barely talked at all.

"So you and my brother…"

Nadia found Sam watching her, chin on her upturned palm, grin spread across her face. "Excuse me?"

"You were looking all dreamy and far away just now. I know that look. I see that look on Ben's face each and every day."

Nadia brought her now lukewarm beer to her mouth while she tried desperately to fashion a response.

"At least I hope it's my brother you're looking so moony about, considering the last time I saw the two of you, you had your tongues entwined."

When Nadia near *choked* on her drink, she put it down carefully then sank her head into her hands, before sliding said hands through her shaggy hair. "What makes you think that was anything but a momentary lapse of reason?"

"I know my brother, Nadia. He's the human version of the skyscrapers he builds—big, strong, invulnerable. This is the first time I've ever seen him so struck he can't hide it and you, my sweet, did the striking."

At that her palms began to sweat, her blood rang in her ears, and she wondered if this was what one of Sam's panic attacks felt like. "Sammy Sam, I don't meant to burst your bubble, but there is *no* your brother and me. Not in the way you mean." She paused, knowing what she was about to say would complicate the simplest friendship of her life. "Melbourne was always a time-out for me, Sam. But that time's run out. In the next few weeks the reps from the new Sky High show are flying out to Australia to see a small contingent of Australian dancers who've been asked to audition by invitation only. I'm one of those dancers."

Sam's face fell, for a second seeming to literally slip down over her bones. "Does Ryder know?"

Nadia swallowed. "I never would have agreed to take on your wedding party account if I wasn't sure I'd be here until all your lessons are done."

Sam's next look was older than her twenty-four years. "That's what's my brother would call being deliberately obtuse."

Nadia breathed out hard and fast. Then threw out her hands in surrender. "No, I don't believe I've mentioned it to him. Or to any of my other students, for that matter."

She sent Sam a pointed glance, which Sam returned in good measure. And rightly so. Nadia hadn't spent a good many hours the evening before naked with any of her *other students*.

So why *had* she with Ryder? What made him so different from the dozen or so clients who'd made advances? Because there had been more. Plenty.

Ryder was beautiful to look at, sure, and unbelievably sexy in a prowling panther kind of way. But she was also fast gathering that he was ambitious and wry, complicated and intense, and while she'd gambled with more than her share of luck over the years he wasn't big on second chances. Maybe that was it—he had the right amount of emotional baggage to draw her to him, like moths to the same flame.

Sam held up a hand at Nadia, halting her mid-thought, before hailing a waiter, ordering more beer, then saying, "I'm going to say one more thing and then that's it, lips zipped shut. And that is Ryder would rather pull out his toenails with tweezers than talk about our father, though he will any time he knows I need to, which is only part of why he's a great guy. Any woman would be lucky to have him in their life. And no matter what's at the end of the road, for this moment in time, Nadia, that woman could be you."

Nadia slid the red paper serviette from around her unused knife and breathed in deep, hoping Sam couldn't see how shaky her breath was. Because in the quiet dark hours of night, she'd gone in circles thinking pretty much the same thing: that here and now didn't have to have anything to do with the near future.

But it did. It always did. She knew better than anyone that past and future were so tightly knotted and profoundly intertwined, if one didn't tread lightly they could strangle you.

"For as long as I can remember all I wanted to do was dance. Then a year ago I had it all—a job I loved, in a city filled with life and excitement and opportunity. And I threw it all away because—" *Because of a guy*, she'd been about to say. But no. She'd come to admit that had only been an excuse. Then why? Because she'd needed to take a breath? Because it had given her the perfect excuse to go running home to Mum? A little bit of all that. But also, "Because I didn't know what I had till it was gone. I've realised since then that life doesn't just happen, you choose it. And I choose dance. I'll always choose dance."

"Dancing means that much?"

"I wouldn't know who I was without it."

The waiter returned, condensation dripping down the brown glass of their beer bottles. When Nadia took the drink from his hand she realised she'd torn the red serviette to pieces.

"Man, I envy your passion." Sam stared at the red mess, before bringing the drink to her mouth. "And enough said. As for the other, apart from the fact that you've just broken my heart a little bit, now we'll have a couch to crash on if we ever get to Vegas, right?"

"For as long as you want."

With that, Sam let out a big sigh then closed her eyes to the rare bout of dry sunshine. Relieved at having told Sam her plans, Nadia tried to do the same. But now that she'd told Sam, now she'd brought that world into this, it somehow made it real. Like in the stars real. And anticipation flowed through her veins like liquid ice till the tips of her fingers tingled as they did when she worked the ropes too long.

As this time she understood the gravity of the opportunity.

Her year away from professional dance had helped her grow up, and it had started the moment she'd knocked on her mother's Toorak door, scoring nothing but a raised eyebrow.

It shouldn't have been a surprise; it was exactly her family's particular brand of solace. Twist an ankle? *Suck it up.* Bomb an audition? *Get over it.* And it certainly shouldn't have hurt so much. Rejection was as much a part of being a dancer as warming up. Still, it had felt like a punch right to her centre, and things had started becoming very clear.

What she wanted more than anything was to dance.

What she *needed* was to do so as far from her mother as humanly possible.

Necessity and desire burned within her and the reality check had just added fuel to the fire. Within the next six weeks she'd have the chance to have it all.

One wrong step and it could all go up in smoke.

Ryder pushed open the door to the dance studio, letting himself in.

After the day he'd had he was glad to be anywhere but on site. Accustomed to the politics of such a substantial and significant project, that day the trivialities had grated to the point he'd felt one problem away from abandoning the whole damn thing.

By contrast the studio was blissfully quiet. The lights dim. Slivers of cool moonlight shone through the bare windows painting patches of white on the scuffed wooden floor. He cast only a perfunctory glance at the beautiful beams above, as he was in pursuit of a different kind of therapy altogether.

It had been three days since that afternoon of delight in Nadia's battered little apartment. Three long days since he'd left her at her door with a long kiss, her face soft with release. Then he'd gone home. Gone to work. And pretended it had been a perfectly normal encounter.

Unfortunately, pretending hadn't made it so.

Normal for him meant no promises, no surprises, taking extreme care to leave no wreckage in his wake. Nadia turned him upside down and inside out until, even while he had no idea what he'd be walking into, or which version of the woman he'd encounter, he'd looked forward to Tuesday night more than anything else that week.

He dumped his gear on the moth-eaten old chair, and looked around. So where the hell was she? The eerie silence built inside him as he walked the wall of windows, anticipation and unrest mixing until his senses keened with every creak of an old floorboard, every shift of dust motes on the sultry air.

"Howdy," Nadia's voice twanged behind him.

Ryder spun on his heels to find her standing by the big old curtains; tiny curls that had escaped from her hair band framing her face, dark eyes a smudge, lush lips hooked into a smile. Her face and neck were dewy from exercise, the rest of her encased in a long-sleeved, cross-over-type top, a short black skirt, fishnet tights, and spiked high heels.

"Nadia," he managed.

Her eyes flickered reproachfully over his suit. "How was work, Ace?"

"Incessant." He'd spent the day battling unions and clients and staff and contractors and suppliers rather than doing any of the hands-on designing that his job was meant to be about. At least he'd thought so once upon a time. "Yours?"

"Hard, actually." She rolled her shoulders and stretched

out a hamstring to bring that home. "Care to see what I've been up to?"

The unsettling inside out and upside down feeling came swarming back, yet he found himself saying, "You bet."

Without another word she whipped back the curtains at the corner of the room revealing…

"Holy mother of…" Ryder said, his feet propelling him forward as his eyes darted from runs of black ropes dripping from the beams above, over wafting swathes of red silk doing the same, to a sparkling silver hula hoop dangling six feet off the floor.

His eyes ran all the way up the heavy-duty wire wrapped about and bolted to the beams above. Architecturally inventive as he was, he was pretty sure he'd never look at a beam the same way again.

"You look a little freaked, my friend."

Ryder flicked a glance to Nadia to find her watching him, her arms folded over her chest. Defensive. And comprehension began to trickle down his spine. So this was how she was going to play it after their afternoon together. His little dance teacher was throwing down the gauntlet.

Schooling his features into the very definition of impassive, Ryder offered up a half-smile. "Dare I ask what it's all for?"

Nadia cocked a hip, all insouciance and grace. It was a heady combination. Especially since he now knew the curve of that hip, knew the taste of that dewy skin, the skill of that lush mouth, the light that shone from those guarded eyes when she was laid bare.

"How about I show you instead?" With that she unhooked her skirt, and nudged off her shoes, leaving her in the long-sleeved top, black bikini bottoms and fishnets. Holy hell.

With practised ease she slid fingerless leather gloves over her palms, snapping studs behind her wrists with an audible click that he felt right in his groin. A small voice inside his head told him to *Run!* A louder voice told him to stay the hell where he was, as he might just have found paradise.

With a few quick stretches, she breathed in, then out, ran the soles of her feet over a towel on the floor, stretched out her fingers, steadied her breath. Then she positioned herself beneath the ropes, taking care as she curled them about her wrists, tugging to—he hoped—check the tension. Then, with a quick glance over her shoulder, she said, "Ready?"

"As I'll ever be."

Her first smile, a glimmer of light in her eyes, she then lifted her feet off the ground and with deft rolls of her arms and flicks of rope behind her knees seemed to float up into the sky.

He'd been fully aware of the grace of her every movement before that moment. He'd danced at her side and in her arms. He'd been inside her and around her and beneath her and above, and been bewitched by the knowledge and control she had over her beautiful body.

But as she turned herself into and out of the grip of the shiny black rope, stopping only for her strong, lithe body to make the most insanely beautiful shapes, all he could think was: *upside down and inside out.*

No music rent the air as she continued her hypnotic routine; the only sounds the hot summer wind whipping against the window, the swish of the ropes as Nadia tumbled through the air, and the thunder of his heart as he stopped himself time and again from reaching out when he thought she might fall.

But she never even came close.

She knew exactly what she was doing.

She was a wonder.

And then she was falling, plummeting, the rope unwinding from around her.

Fear hurled into Ryder's throat, until she planted a foot on the floor; her ponytail swishing across her neck as her body came to a halt. Her chest rising and falling. Tousled hair matted to her neck with perspiration. Eyes burning into his as if daring him to even try to think himself worthy of such a creature.

But for the first time in his life Ryder didn't give a flying hoot if he was worthy. He was a mass of pure instinct. Of need and fear and hunger; all of it primal, uncoiling from deep down inside, reaching out with perfect aim.

Nadia twirled her hands back into the rope till her arms were stretched up straight. "What did you think?"

As if she weren't fully aware blood was pumping so hard and fast through Ryder's body he could barely think at all. "If that's part two of the routine I've been sent here to learn," he said, his rough voice echoing across the huge space, "then Sam can think again."

Surprise flared in her dark eyes before Nadia laughed, the sound soft, husky.

Her fingers flexed, as if she was about to let go. But Ryder shook his head, infinitesimally, little more than a private wish. Then, after a long hot thick moment in which Ryder's blood rushed like a river between his ears, she instead rolled the rope higher, trapping her hands further, the stretch revealing a sliver of skin between her top and pants.

When she tilted her chin, she might as well have said, *Come and get it.* He didn't need to be asked twice.

Three long strides ate up the distance between them and then his hands were on her cheeks, his mouth on hers. The ropes swung her away from him, but he followed, ravenous, already pushed beyond the edge of reason.

His kisses moved to her neck, her throat, and then he was on his knees, not caring what the dust and old floorboards would do to his suit trousers. He had a million suits. There was only one Nadia, strapped up for his pleasure. And hers.

When he gripped her hips, she arched into him, again revealing a sliver of that delicious hard belly. He ran a thumb across the pale crescent, marvelling in the way her skin tightened, her muscles twitched. He followed with his mouth, running a trail of kisses in the wake of his touch, the scent of her filling his nostrils.

He looked up to find her watching him. Waiting. Anticipation kicking at the corner of her mouth. Desire flaring thick and fast behind her eyes. And something else. Defiance. As if they were playing on her terms.

And something came over him, a deep-rooted need to tame, to possess, to show her who was boss.

To negate his father's cavalier blood, Ryder had spent his entire life trying to be the most civilised man he knew. But this woman— One look, one cock of her hip, one tilt of her mouth, she simply stripped him bare.

Like a devil's whisper, it filtered through the haze of desire that if he gave her an inch this woman could well tear him apart. But it was too late.

He nudged her feet apart with his knees. She resisted, instinct kicking in. Too bad.

It was his turn to lead.

Eyes on hers, he slowly, achingly slowly, rolled the waistline of her pants and stockings down. Her mouth slid open to drag in breaths that were harder to come by. She tried biting her bottom lip, to retain control, but when he felt the trembling, heard it in the escape of a moan, he knew it was a lost cause.

When her tights hit her knees, he slid his hands up the backs of her thighs, desire knotting his gut as her head dropped back, her knees gave way, and the only thing holding her up was the rope biting into her wrists.

When his hands reached her backside, he breathed her in, desire pressing him near to the brink of control. Then he took her in his mouth, licking, nibbling, nudging, sucking, as she rocked and pitched and writhed above him.

When her trembling reached fever pitch, with one final deep lick he sent her over the edge. Feeling the strength in her sweet body, the tension in her arms, the utter freedom in her release, knowing he'd done that to her, this superwoman, was the single sexiest moment of his life.

He didn't wait for her to come down before he was on his feet, his hands making short work of her tantalising top, yanking it from her shoulder, needing more, needing to taste all of her, to imprint her flavour on his psyche and himself all over every damn inch of her.

No finessing, he took her breast into his mouth, hard, gripping her waist as she cried out from the new pleasures rolling through her. She hooked her legs around him, pulling him close.

Ryder glanced at the beams. His voice subterranean, he asked, "Can they hold the both of us?"

"We'll soon find out," she said, before taking his mouth with hers.

So hard he hurt, he freed himself, somehow found the cognitive wherewithal to protect himself. Silently berating her for not insisting, hating himself for liking that she hadn't, he pressed into her, hard, relishing every sensational second.

Her eyes snapped shut and she cried out. The muscles in her arms and neck strained, beads of sweat beaded all over her chest, curls tight around her face. Her beautiful face. And the sweet bliss of being inside her, pleasure riding him as he stroked into her; hoping they weren't about to bring the building down around their ears.

All too soon her climax came hard. Curling her into him as she cried out. While his built from a tight knot of need that unfurled until he felt it to the ends of his everything.

And he came with a roar that shook the foundations of the old building till the thing near rained down dust.

Her head dropped to his shoulder, her breaths fanning against his ear, and he held her there, still inside her, their heartbeats slamming against one another as they drifted back to earth.

Ryder lowered her feet to the floor and since her hands were out of action he gently rolled her tights back into place. He uncurled one rope then the other, the red raw ligature marks making him wince. Then when her legs seemed about to give way, he scooped her into his arms. Ryder carried her to the lounge, where he sat. She sank into him, soft and warm, her head beneath his chin, her hand on his heart. The quiet afterglow washed over him, as a warmth in his muscles and a sweet ache in his groin.

Then, just when her breaths grew so slow and heavy he wondered if she'd fallen asleep, she spoke up, her voice, soft and shattered, said, "Ryder?"

He wiped damp hair from her forehead. "Yes, Nadia?"

"I'm leaving."

"I'd like to see you try."

Her fingers curled into his chest a moment before she lifted her heavy head and looked up into his eyes. And the distress that flittered therein made his gut constrict—more than ropes, or studded gloves, or high heels that could castrate a man with one well-positioned step.

Then she said, "That routine was part of an audition piece I've been working on. Sky High, the company I used to work for, are casting a new show. And I'm on the shortlist." She paused to swallow. "If I get the job—*when* I get the job—as soon as humanly possible I'll be moving there."

"Where's *there* exactly?"

"Vegas."

"As in *Las* Vegas?" *The other side of the world.*

Her mouth twitched. "Is there any other?"

"Good point."

Truth was, he had no idea what he was saying; he was marking time. Dammit, his skin still thrummed from some of the hottest sex of his life. He couldn't think forward an hour much less weeks.

"Vegas," he echoed again. And as the ripples fanned to the corner of his mind, so many things began to make sense. Her reticence to make good on their attraction. Her drab apartment. She'd not put down roots because she'd never intended to stay.

"When?" he asked.

The flicker in her eyes making it clear she knew he'd been sideswiped. Damn. "They're en route now, but it depends how many dancers they decide to see in each place before they get here. I'm just waiting for the word."

She said it with a smile. Yet it was Nadia's complete stillness that got to him. Any other time even her very breaths moved through her as if she were dancing, yet she sat in his arms so still, so inert, she might as well have been made of air. Because this conversation was that important to her. Or that uncomfortable. Whatever it was to her, it clearly carried weight. *He* carried weight.

"Okay, then," he said.

It must have been the right answer, as her sinuous body settled deeper into his lap. He dragged his thumb gently over her lower lip and when she lifted her face to his followed with a kiss.

A kiss filled with sweetness, and tenderness, yet humming with heat.

And as his desire ratcheted up faster than ought to have been physiologically possible, he knew her imminent departure from his life was a blessing in disguise. He clearly couldn't keep away from her even if he wanted to. This woman who so effortlessly lured him into temptation. Who made him clamour to tap into the darkness, the consuming desires, the inner storm he'd all but eliminated from his life.

As for Nadia? There was no getting away from the look in her eyes as she'd told him she was going away. He'd glimpsed that look before in the rare moments when she let her guard down, when she'd unexpectedly opened up to him, when she'd forgotten to be on show and simply was.

A woman like *that* needed a different kind of man in her life. Not a man who worked more hours than not. Not a man with the complicated responsibilities he had. Not a man who'd never confuse lust for forever. And damn sure not a Fitzgerald.

CHAPTER SEVEN

NADIA STRETCHED OUT her limbs and groaned; the slide of soft sheets over her body as lovely as her all-over ache was wicked. Her body was used to being pushed to the edge of endurance and then some, but the past couple of weeks with Ryder had educated her as to muscles even *she* never knew existed.

She tilted her head to find the man himself sleeping on his back, the crumpled sheet covering one thigh and half his torso, moonlight pouring through his bedroom window over the hard dips and planes of his body, glinting off the dark hair covering the gentle rise and fall of his chest, the heat of him warming even her side of his bed.

Watching him, this man who took her places she'd never before been, her hands circled her wrists, rubbing at marks that had faded days before. She'd underestimated Ryder in giving him a private dance. Expected him to be dissuaded by her stunts. She'd also overestimated her own willpower, as every day since, every time she was with him she told herself it would be the last, her resolve caved.

Her fault probably, for unlocking the danger junkie in him. How could she have known that beneath the slick suits he was so audacious, a sensualist, fearless? That she'd be the one left gasping, breathless, and shaken again and again and again.

The twin threads keeping her sane as they embarked on

this impossible affair were the countdown to Sam's wedding and her impending audition. Not that they talked about the fact that their association had a big brick wall looming at its end, but they hadn't needed to; the ticking clock was simply there.

With a sigh she lifted her gaze to the two-storey wall of glass that filled the far side of Ryder's floating bedroom as well as the entire beach-side wall of the floor beneath. She guessed it was past midnight. Time to leave if she wanted some sleep.

Slipping from the bed, her toes curling against the plush rug, Nadia quietly gathered her clothes and got dressed. She nearly gave up on finding her strappy high heels before she saw them peeking out from under Ryder's side of the bed; by request they'd been the last item left on.

With the straps hooked over one finger, she took one last look at the big man sleeping in the big bed; his lips softly parted, dark hair falling over his forehead, the shadow of stubble already covering his cheeks and chin. When all that masculine warmth made her start to ache, she resolutely turned her back and walked away.

She texted for a cab as she padded down the circular staircase to the main floor of Ryder's amazing home. He'd designed the space himself—and for himself *alone*; that much was clear. All hardwood floors, and raw slate tiles, dark grey walls and sleek modern furniture. Downstairs was entirely open-plan with a sophisticated kitchen and a gigantic lounge that made the most of the beach views, with a cool art-deco bar and a TV you could see from space. Ryder had alluded to a garage, gym, and laundry in the subterranean floor below.

The only thing in the place that wasn't uber-masculine was a truly lovely antique-looking drafting table in the far corner. A more modern chair was skewed beneath and the wall beside it housed a wall of built-in blond bookshelves filled with rolled-up plans and books galore—all the accoutrements she assumed an architect must need.

And yet for all the modern, manly minimalism—the reclaimed wood, re-imagined steel, the huge artworks on the mood-lit walls that all seemed to be made from industrial cast-offs—the place was truly stunning.

He'd mentioned that his mother had been creative, a sculptor of some renown. No wonder Ryder Fitzgerald had talent; he had the heart of an artist.

Nadia snorted softly at her wayward thoughts, figuring she must be more tired than she thought. She dragged her hair into a ponytail, tugging her hair a little harder than necessary in order to wake herself up. Last stop, she ducked to the fridge, found an apple to appease her empty stomach—since they'd somehow forgotten to eat.

Padding towards the door, she sank her teeth into the skin, and a resounding snap of apple flesh split the air.

She stilled and heard the distinct rustle of sheets over man.

Swearing beneath her breath, she gathered her satchel from its place hooked over the back of a bar stool, then clamped the apple between her teeth and made a barefoot run for the door.

She'd almost made it when the floorboards creaked ominously. Heart thundering in her chest, she took the apple from her mouth and glanced back to find Ryder ambling down the stairs; his hair dishevelled, his face soft with sleep. Previously discarded suit trousers covered his long legs, the clasp undone revealing the tantalising arrow of dark hair.

He stopped when he spotted her hand on the doorknob. "I thought I heard you decamping," he said, his voice deep and soft on the night air.

"You heard right. I also stole an apple."

He crossed his arms and leant a hip against the railing. "Consider it yours."

Nadia's pulse thudded at her wrists, behind her ears. All over. As even while he looked perfectly relaxed, she could feel the slumberous desire rolling from him in waves. And even while the muscle memory in her body begged her to make good on all that promise, she needed to be sure that when the time came, she *could* say no.

"See you Tuesday night?" she asked.

A beat throbbed between them before he said, "I'll be there."

He shifted, and her skin thrummed with the thought there might be one last kiss; a deep, sweet, lasting parting meeting of mouths that took her breath away. But one dark look later, he gave her a short nod and headed back up the stairs.

The tension drained from her until she drooped like a wilting flower. She let herself out, the cool darkness and soft salty tang of the sea air enveloping her. And then she began to laugh. It was either that or sob with relief. Or would that be disappointment? Argh!

And when her cab swished to a halt at the kerb, she hopped inside, settled against the seat and closed her eyes, smiling until her cheeks began to ache.

As Ryder hit the stairs leading up to the studio the next Tuesday night, he heard Nadia's laughter echoing down the stairwell.

He was smiling by the time he pushed open the door, but at the creak of the hinges she spun on her heel, her hand flying to her chest, her cheeks glowing pink, her phone pressed to her ear. A couple of beats later she held up a finger, mouthing she'd only be a minute, then turned her back, talked in a low hum he couldn't make out.

Ryder dumped his bags on the couch and headed her

way. He slid his arms around her waist, and ducked his face into her neck.

Frowning furiously, she tried to peel him away, to motion that she was on the phone.

He merely grabbed the offending hand and held it behind her, trapping it between them. He slid his other hand down the neck of her top until he found her breast, the hot sweet weight of it filling his palm and making him groan.

When he caught their reflection in the window, his hand down her top, her mouth open, her eyes hot and hard, he dipped his head to take her ear lobe in his mouth, not taking his eyes from her mirror image.

Then, husky as all get out, she said, "Thanks for the heads-up. Talk soon," and hung up the phone.

She pressed her sweet backside into him and curled the hand holding the phone around his neck to pull his mouth to hers for a long lush kiss. Heat thundered through him, making his whole world a tight sweet ache.

Eyes locked onto her shadowy likeness in the window, he peeled her top away to reveal her breast to the air, her skin so pale and sweet against the tan of his big hand. She shivered, her eyes fluttering closed, her head rocking back against his shoulder.

He grazed her nipple with his thumb, and again as it pebbled beneath his touch. Her tongue snuck out to wet her lips. She might as well have licked him lower for the kick of heat that knocked the breath right out of him—

Ryder leapt away from her as music blasted right next to his ear. Rubbing at his ear, he glared towards the offending noise to see the phone still gripped in Nadia's hand.

Already hooking her top back in place first, Nadia switched it to silent. "Sorry."

He tilted his chin to the phone gripped in her hand. "Miss Popular tonight."

"Hmm?" She blinked as if the lit-up phone weren't still vibrating in her palm.

Which was when Ryder felt a frisson of disquiet scoot down his spine. "You going to answer it?"

She shook her head. "No need."

"Why's that?"

"I know what it's about."

"Seriously, Nadia, you want to play twenty questions? Or tell me what's going on?"

A frown flickered across her brow and was gone just as fast. Then she lifted stubborn eyes to his. "The producers will be here in a little over a week. And I don't even have to go to Sydney, as they're coming to Melbourne. They're coming to me."

She didn't have to say which producers. Her return to her old life had been hovering between them since the night she'd told him it was on the cards. And after the initial bombshell it had morphed into something far more constructive: a neat little end point to the affair. And yet as it coalesced from an insubstantial notion into a concrete event everything inside Ryder distilled down to two thoughts: *one week* and *too soon*.

So immersed in his own reaction, he hadn't noticed that Nadia wasn't looking at him. Her cheeks were unusually pale, and her knuckles had gone white around the phone. He'd seen her fierce. He'd seen her near belligerent. He'd seen her sweet and soft and he'd seen her surrender. But he'd never seen Nadia Kent worry about a single damn thing.

He closed in and slid his fingers through her hair, lifting her head till she was looking him in the eye; the tumble of emotions ricocheting through her slid right into him. All he could do was hold on tight and barricade himself against the tide. "You okay?"

Her jaw clenched beneath his fingers as she lifted her

chin, denial in her every movement. But he knew her, intimately. And from one blink to the next he saw her—the real Nadia, the raw Nadia, the one who'd yanked him from the safe side of the ravine to the other. The side where he wasn't in control of his actions. His thoughts. His desires. The Nadia that could only lead him into disaster. And yet he couldn't look away.

"You're nervous," he said as realisation dawned.

"Of course I'm bloody nervous! I hardly proved myself reliable the last time I worked for them, so I'm coming at this with my chances hobbled from the outset. And what if I screw it up? What if I'm not in as good condition as I think I am? I haven't had to choreograph on my own for years—what if the routine sucks?"

He ran both thumbs over her temples. "I've witnessed your work, remember. Hottest damn thing I've ever seen. If they won't pay you to perform it, I will. Hang on a sec, I already did."

She laughed, and then slapped him on the arm. He grabbed her hand and held it behind her.

Her eyes turned wild. Rebellious.

So he slid his other hand through her hair, cradling the back of her head, holding her in thrall. Then he dipped his mouth to brush hers. When she didn't react, he kissed her again, barely a touch, then a luxurious swipe of his tongue across the seam. He felt her acquiescence in her melting body a fraction before she finally opened her mouth to him, sliding her tongue against his in a dance they both knew so well.

The kiss grew intense, heated, sumptuous, long. So long, when they finally pulled apart Ryder couldn't quite catch his breath. And—by the way Nadia's eyes flickered back and forth between his—he was pretty certain she felt the same way.

And yet she was leaving. Extremely soon. And while

every impulse was to squeeze every last drop of passion from their affair that he could, he knew the level-headed move was to begin the gentle withdraw gracefully. Before anybody got hurt.

Ryder spun her about and gave her a little shove in the opposite direction. "Come on, Teach. You're not the only one with a countdown till the day you have to set the dance world on fire. The guests at the Fitzgerald-Johnson nuptials will not be disappointed."

She shot him a dark glance over her shoulder, but when he didn't give her what she was looking for she rolled her shoulder, morphed into teacher mode. And gave Ryder one of the hardest workouts he'd ever had.

On their way out Ryder saw the extra bag he'd brought that he'd completely forgotten about in all the excitement. He thought about leaving it forgotten, but in the end he silently handed it over.

"For me?" Nadia took the bag and poked her head inside. She blinked. "Apples."

"I saw them and thought of you."

When she looked up her eyes were wide, and there was no hiding the flush that had risen to her cheeks. "But I only owed you one—now I owe you a tree."

"And don't think I don't have every intention of collecting on the debt. Before you leave," he added as he held open the door leading outside the building.

"The man's all charm. How will I ever survive the parting?" she said, voice dripping with sarcasm.

Yet the glance she shot him as she slid past him was not. It was quick; it was fleeting. It was *yearning*. And it had had nothing to do with what was ahead of her, and everything to do with him.

Ryder swung his keys around a finger as he opened up the passenger side of his car, trying to ignore it. The look, the way it had landed right in his centre with a thud, the way this woman managed to make his well-shackled ego roar to life.

Till she was about to slide inside. Then he whipped an arm across the door, blocking her way. His voice was subterranean as he asked, “Think you’ll miss me when you head off to the bright lights of Sin City?”

Her eyes widened a fraction, her pupils swamping her dark irises in a red-hot instant. Then she shrugged and said, *“Meh.”*

His ego growled at the challenge. “You scoff now, Miss Kent, but just hope I don’t really turn on the charm. You might never bring yourself to leave.”

She breathed in hard, seeming to suck away all the air around them, and all the dangerous teasing of the past few minutes compressed until they were suddenly locked in their own personal pressure cell.

“Ryder.” Her voice was deep, vibrating, but tinged with warning. “I will leave. I *have* to.”

“I know that,” said Ryder.

Her brow creased into a series of little frowns. Then, just before she slipped into her car, she said, “I will miss you though.”

Hell. “Right back at ya, kid.”

The ride back to his place was quiet.

“Crap!”

“Problem?” Ryder asked, glancing up from reading the “paper” on his tablet.

Nadia was settled on his couch wearing one of his T-shirts, glaring at his laptop perched on her bare legs. He’d woken that morning to find her still curled into his arms. The first time she hadn’t snuck out during the night. It seemed he wasn’t the only one debating the benefit of getting as much out of their last days together as they could.

She dug her fingers into her hair. "No. Yes. I don't know."

"Anything I can do?"

She pinned him with a dark look that didn't bode well. "Not unless you have any Mafia links."

"For what purpose?"

"I might be in need of a hit man."

Right. "I work in construction. What do you think?"

Her eyes widened and lost the dark clouds for a few seconds as she took that in, but they slowly slid back in. Then she lay back on the couch, an arm flung elegantly over her eyes, her feet hooked over the back rest.

"Nadia, you're currently more intriguing than today's news but I *am* about to hit the entertainment section..."

One eye poked out. "Nope. Don't want to demystify your elevated opinion of me."

When her feet began to point and flex coquettishly over the back of his couch, Ryder pressed himself away from his chair and went to join her. It didn't take much. "And what, pray tell, does this elevated opinion entail exactly?"

"That I'm formidable and focused and fabulous."

That pretty much covered it.

"Don't get me wrong," she said, hidey arm forgotten as she tilted her gorgeous face to him. "I am *all* of that."

"And more."

"Thank you."

"But..."

"I'm freaking out right now."

When her feet began to shake up and down, as if trying to lose excess energy through her toes, he knew she wasn't exaggerating. "Why?"

"Because I'd naturally assumed he'd be travelling to Europe with the old show, so never gave him a second thought. But I just got an email about the audition tour, and he's been listed as coming. Here. To watch me dance. I'm screwed. I'm royally screwed."

"*He* being?"

"My ex." She pulled herself upright and gave the laptop a little shove, tilting it his way. Ryder got a glimpse of a man with brown hair, pale skin, smouldering blue eyes. The fact that Nadia's lip curled as she said his name somewhat mollified Ryder's urge to rearrange those pretty-boy features but good.

"Associate producer, I see. You lost your job while he got promoted."

"So it seems. He always knew how to play the game. The woman—and she was barely that—he left me for was the niece of one of the producers. I, on the other hand, was dancing under another name so as *not* to cash in on my connections. And now look at us." Her tone was snappy but her body was so expressive he knew she was more upset than she was letting on. "There's also the fact that he is a brilliant dancer. One of those born with that elusive "X" factor. Stage presence like—"

"How could you bear to leave such a creature behind?"

Nadia didn't even have the good grace to blush. When her eyes skewed to his her mouth stretched into a knowing smile. "If I didn't know better I'd say you sounded jealous."

"Lucky you know better."

"Mmm."

When her gaze swept back to the laptop, caught on the image smouldering back at her, all humour faded and she shut it closed with a snap. Then she ran her hands over her face, before hunching and staring through the wall of windows to the sparkling water views beyond.

"If he has hiring rights, which is how it reads, then this ups the ante big time. I'm going to have to pull out all the stops." She swallowed, hard, then, "The entire time I worked for them they had no idea who my mother was. But what if letting it be known made the difference this time—" She nibbled at her bottom lip. "Because the thought of not getting this job…"

Her hand fisted into her T-shirt—which was actually his—lifting it from the long legs draped over the couch. How could she not know she had so much charisma, so much instant sex appeal she'd only have to saunter into that room and any producer worth his salt would hire her on the spot?

That bloody mother of hers had a lot to answer for.

"Nadia," he near growled.

"Mmm?"

"Nadia, look at me."

For once she did as she was told.

"Don't do it," he said.

An initial burst of shock lit her eyes before they narrowed. Like where did he get the right to have an opinion at all? He didn't care much if he had the right or not, she was going to have to hear what he had to say.

"You got where you were despite her once before. You can do it again."

"Sweet sentiment, Ryder. But you don't know that."

The number of people Ryder was certain he could count on in his life could be tallied on one hand. Less. Which was why he ran his behemoth business—from the plans to the paper clips—like a mini-monocracy. But in that moment he knew he could count on Nadia. To be true. To do her best. To aim as high as the sky. Because not only was she stunning, provocative, and slippery, she was brave, and gutsy, and honourable.

"When it comes to you, Nadia Kent, I most certainly do."

She swallowed. Then hooked her thumbnail against a tooth, a soft pink flush rising in her cheeks. "While you, Ryder Fitzgerald, might just be the most surprising man I've ever met."

When the intensity in her arresting eyes began to bring on that upside down inside out feeling, he ducked his chin to the simpering sap on the laptop. "All evidence to the contrary."

Yet her eyes remained on his. It was a long moment, a heady moment, before she glanced away and said, "Yeah. And you're right about the other thing too. A moment of weakness averted. Bugger it. It just means my routine will have to be so amazing, so beyond the edge of anything they've ever seen, they'll have to hire me."

She uncurled herself from the chair and shook out her whole body. Ryder's eyes roved over her mane of unkempt hair, her sexy bare feet with the faint crisscross of old rope burns and the sparkly hipster G-string under that T-shirt of his. She far from harmonised with the minimalist décor of his home. So why did she look so damn good inside it?

It hit him that it wouldn't be much longer before he'd no longer have this view to look forward to. No more of that soft, sweet warmth to smooth the edges off his busy days. No more of that spitting, sparking heat to set fire to his spacious bed. No more fogged-up bathroom after her decadently long hot showers. No more missing fruit. No more Nadia.

Glad she'd stayed, he reached out and snagged her hips, catching her off balance so she fell into him. Laughing, she settled her thighs over his, shuffling till she was more comfortable, till he was anything but.

He slid a hand into her hair. Laughter lit her eyes, laughter and enquiry. When he ran a thumb down her cheek, tangling his fingers in that wild voluptuous hair, the laughter dried up. And he once again caught that touch of yearning.

And he knew he wasn't the only one now counting the days, the hours, wondering which kiss would be their last.

Nadia pressed her lips to his neck; it was so welcome he groaned. She kissed him again, more, until kisses rained all over his cheeks, his ear lobe, his collarbone. Her tongue following in their wake, warm and terrible in the reactions it invoked. The need, the tension, building and burning inside him, impossible and everything all at once.

Then gentle hands found his buttons and opened them one by one. Slow enough he felt each pop like something unhooking inside him.

Her touch was reverent, her mouth searching. The yearning not locked away this time, but right there. Every kiss honest and real, peeling away the layers of reluctance he'd spent years building. And by the time she laid his shirt open, she'd laid him bare.

He could feel his heart beating, not only in his chest, but in his wrists, in his feet, at the back of his head, as if a tornado were trapped behind his skin.

Then her mouth was on his chest, her lips following the rises, her tongue dipping sweetly into the falls, before her teeth closed over his nipple, biting down. It lasted a second, probably less, but the shock of it was like a dagger in his thorax.

He swallowed down the pain, owning it. He had to if he had any intention of enduring this as she slid his shirt from his shoulders and kissed him there. Her hands running down the flats of his blades, her fingers tracing his spine, spanning his waist till every muscle clenched with the sweet agony of her touch.

It was unbearable. Ryder clenched his teeth till his head rang from it.

And when her hands moved to slide under his backside, her mouth slanting over his, he gave up and took it. Took it all. He'd suffer the guilt another day. Right then he was too far gone to care.

In one swift move, he flipped her onto her back, her hair falling in waves across the cushions, her eyes bright, her luscious lips slick. And he made love to her right there.

Slowly, gently, eyes on hers the entire time. Feelings sweeping through so strong him he could barely breathe.

Nadia came with a swift rise of heat, her neck arching, her hands gripping his arms, her mouth sliding open with sweet pleasure. And as she hit her peak his followed, pleasure riveting him inside and out, for the longest time, until he thought it might clear knock him out.

And then in a shudder of limbs and sighs they tumbled into afterglow. Together.

Her hand dove into the hair at the back of his neck, and she pressed herself closer, as if searching for an anchor. He felt it too; the wreckage, the insanity, the irrationality of how good they were together. How frustratingly perfect. It reverberated through him. Like a warning. Like a huge calamitous siren that any rational person would know meant go back, do not enter.

Danger lurked behind that door. The kind he'd long since vowed he'd never risk. And yet there'd been a moment back there when he'd shoved aside reason, knowing he was about to knock on that door hard enough to split the thing right down the middle.

Gripping onto his last tattered vestiges of sense, Ryder pulled himself away from her.

"Come on," said Ryder, taking her hand in his to haul her limp, soft, stunning body from his couch.

"Come on what?"

"Just come on."

"Don't you have to go to work?"

"Not today." He did, of course. But he wouldn't. For the first time in his life he was blowing off work. Today, it seemed, was a day of breaking rules.

"So where are we going?"

Anywhere but here. Anything but this.

"You'll see."

CHAPTER EIGHT

WHICH WAS HOW Nadia ended up on the side of a long straight road leading to the Yarra Valley, sitting in the driver's seat of Ryder's charming vintage coupe. Though from her vantage point, with all the old-fashioned dials and lights and pedals clogging her vision, the thing looked anything but charming. It looked positively petrifying.

Hands levitating an inch off the steering wheel she turned to glare at him. "You're kidding, right?"

"Not, in fact."

"But I told you I can't do this."

"I never thought I'd hear the word can't come out of that mouth."

"Well, you heard it here. Can't. Cannot. Unable. Now let's go. To the beach. I have a bikini that'll make your jaw drop—"

"If seventeen-year-old boys who don't even know how to pull their own pants high enough to cover their asses can drive a car, then so can you."

Nadia muttered a few things about seventeen-year-old boys and the men they turned into, before facing front. He'd pulled her out of the most intense bliss of her life for *this*?

She looked obstinately into the rear-view mirror as the gently winding country road stretched behind her. The lanes were wide, with plenty of space to pull over. They'd been sitting there for five minutes and not a single car had gone by. And yet at the mere thought of driving, she came out in a cold sweat.

Which was ridiculous, really, considering what she did for a living. She'd long since proven she wasn't afraid of anything: heights, rebuff, pain.

All she could put it down to was that she was in some kind of delayed shock about her ex. Because while she'd thought she'd handled the news with about as much aplomb as any person could be expected to, seeing his face, knowing she'd soon see him, had rattled her.

But *this* was more than rattled. At the thought of attempting this thing with Ryder sitting there watching her like a hawk, her throat went crazy dry.

She looked over the bucket seats into the tiny back bench seat of the two-door beast, then back at Ryder. "Ever had sex back there?"

"Don't change the subject."

Nadia bit her lip and faced front. "Shouldn't I read the manual first? Or practise in a simulator of some sort?"

Ignoring her, Ryder went on, "Like most things in life the best way to learn how to drive is by simply doing it."

"What if we crash? What if I roll the car and we die in a burning inferno?"

"Then you can tell me you told me so."

"Don't you have a smaller car? Something a little less magnificent?"

That hooked his attention. Finally! "I thought you didn't think my car all that fancy."

"It's grown on me. And at some point I might have looked it up on Google, you know, in case I one day did want a car. Turns out I'd have to sell a kidney, and a lung, for the privilege of owning one of these babies. I took it as a sign."

He laughed, the sound filling the car with its husky gorgeousness. Nadia looked to him in appeal.

"Stop being such a wimp, Nadia, and do it already. Turn the damn key."

"I'm not a wimp! I'm stronger than I look. I'll prove it. Get out of the car. I'll lift you off your feet right now."

Her hand went to the door handle, but he reached over and locked the door. There his arm remained, pressing her to the back of the seat, the heat of him burning across her chest. But it was his eyes, his stunning hazel eyes, and his voice, smooth and sexy, that had her pinned as he asked, "What are you so afraid of?"

"Not a damn thing!" she said, but even as the words came out of her mouth she knew he was right. She *was* afraid; heart beating in her throat, prickly-skinned, blurry-visioned scared out of her mind. So it was a blessed relief when, like a familiar security blanket, her mother's voice slipped all too easily inside her head: *Grow a spine, kid.*

"Ryder, no, I've had enough—"

"You can do it," Ryder said, his voice deep, demanding, but most of all indulgent, and the anaesthetic dogma that had protected Nadia for so many years simply failed to work.

And through the chink in her armour, she saw, with a flash of insight, what she'd been trying to disregard. She'd never feared being rebuffed by a panel of experts looking for a very specific person to fill a dance role. That was their prerogative. But rejection by someone she respected, someone she trusted, someone she admired…

Ryder. This current craziness was about Ryder.

She pressed her eyes shut tight and swallowed hard. But there was no stopping the feelings, the knowledge, now they'd been set free. She cared what he thought, he mattered to *her*, and she didn't want him to see her fail.

Because at some point in the past few weeks, she'd dropped her guard. Maybe because the auditions were so close. Maybe it was the fact that it was hard to be impervious when completely blissed out by afterglow and you felt as if you'd been melted from the inside out. Whatever the reason, even with her eyes closed, when she breathed in and caught Ryder's masculine scent her heart skittered against her ribs, heat slithered below her skin, and she felt jittery and feverish, and yet somehow at ease. Things she'd never felt before. Not with the same purity, the same effortlessness. Because she'd been taught very early on in life to press all her feelings deep down inside. The bad *and* the good.

Give a damn and they'll eat you alive.

And the second she stopped pushing it all back down, it bubbled up until she felt it all—the breakdown of the first, real, long-term relationship of her adult life, her mother's cruel reaction, the senseless flight from the career she adored. She'd honestly thought she'd taken it all on the chin, but she'd only pressed it down, the whole big hot mess that had led her to that point, spilling into her nerves, her heart, until she couldn't breathe.

"Nadia."

Ryder's voice hummed through her like a tuning fork. She shook her head, no. No. No! Formidable and focused and fabulous, she was invulnerable. But she felt so raw her skin might as well have been flayed from her chest.

Unfortunately he was made of as stern a stuff as she. He grabbed her by the chin, turning her head to face him. She looked at the neckline of his T-shirt instead.

At her obstinacy he laughed—laughed!—before saying, "You asked me to let you lead on the dance floor, and I deferred to you once I grudgingly admitted you had the wisdom of experience over me. I've been driving for well over a decade. Not a single traffic violation to my name. Defer to me, Nadia. Trust me."

She let out a roar of frustration and shook the steering wheel some, but this time didn't let it go. Trapped, panic-stricken, she lifted her eyes to his, all set to tell him to bite her. But the moment her eyes found his, she jammed up. Those eyes. So deep, so beautiful, so patient. And so damn smart.

As if he knew. As if he'd known for some time that she'd been in denial about how quickly she'd gotten over the multiple layers of embarrassment and pain of the events of months past. All she could hang onto was the hope that that was *all* he'd deduced she was in denial about.

At least she'd learnt one thing from events past—the only way out of any mess was through. Nadia breathed in deep and breathed out shaky, happy right then to be breathing at all. "Okay," she said. "Tell me what I have to do?"

"Foot on the clutch," he said. "Gear into First. Key's in the ignition. Turn it right, wait till the engine hums and let go."

Sweat prickling down her back, Nadia followed Ryder's instructions as best she could. And the car bunny-hopped a few feet before wobbling to an ignominious stop. Heat landed in her cheeks with a humiliating thud. "I totally suck."

"Nobody gets the waltz right first go."

"I did."

"And I've never stalled. Duck to water."

At that she laughed; shocked blissful laughter that shaved the sharpest edges off her agitation. With a slow breath out, she resettled herself, went to that quiet place she went before a routine: darkness, silence. Not discounting the natural fear, harnessing it.

In the quiet she heard Ryder's litany of instructions, and, after a few more false starts, the directions began to blend from one move to the next, until it all seemed to click and she was easing out onto the road proper, rural scenery sliding past the window.

"I'm driving!"

"Yes, you are."

"It's easy!"

"Look at the road. Not me."

She swung back to face the road to find herself veering. She nudged the car straight, her eyes on the horizon as he'd taught her. She pressed a little harder on the accelerator, adrenalin spiking as she was pressed back in the seat. "How far can I go?"

"Do you have a learner's permit?"

"What?" Nadia said, her hands flinging off the wheel and feet off the pedals in panic. "Of course not."

The engine stalled and with an oath, Ryder grabbed the wheel and shifted it a fraction so they could ease off the side of the road, where he yanked the parking brake. "Then we'd better stay away from town. And schools, and police, and people in general."

His voice was rough, but when she looked at him he was smiling.

While Nadia let out a "Woop!" of pure delight and laughed till her sides hurt. Relief and joy spilling through her unstoppered. And like a street after a rainstorm, all the muck that had flooded to the surface before had been washed away leaving her feeling shiny and new. "That was awesome. And even better for being illicit, right? What next?"

"Next we lunch. I'm driving." Ryder got out of the car and motioned she do the same.

Lunch? He wanted to *eat*? She was so wired she could fly! Nadia gripped the wheel a moment longer and wondered how far she might get if she just took off. When he opened her door she squinted up at him. "Bonnie and Clyde had to start somewhere."

He merely held out a hand. She let him help her out of the car when she realised she was trembling all over, adrenalin knocking about her insides till her nerves sang. He must have felt it as he cupped her elbows in an effort to steady her, which was kind of sweet. Then his eyes turned dark and he pressed her back against the sloping side of the car which was anything but sweet. "Tell me how that felt?"

Shaking hands running over his chest, she said, "You were the one putting your life in my hands. How did *that* feel?"

His eyes narrowed. "Not in the least bit unusual."

"Oh," Nadia said in barely a whisper. While in the cocoon of the car she'd managed to just hold herself together while being cracked apart. Now, out in the open air, the country breeze tickling at her hair, sunshine pouring down over her bare shoulders, Ryder's challenging hazel eyes looking deep into her own, she felt…too much.

Heat rising, everywhere, she looked up at him. "I know I was a bit of a beast to start with, but thank you for today."

"It just seemed like a nice day for a drive."

Said the man who worked so hard that he never had time to change out of his suit for a ten p.m. appointment, who'd taken a day off because he'd seen she was about to crack and chose to be there to hold her together when she did. "Come on, Ryder," she said with an unsteady laugh. "I doubt you've done a thing in your life that wasn't entirely deliberate."

Something slid behind his eyes like quicksilver, something deep and onerous. "So I might have had an ulterior motive."

His gaze slipped to her neck, the hot spot below her ear, before landing on her lips, and any breath she'd managed to gather in her lungs poured out of her in a shaky sigh. Then his eyes slid back to hers. "You, Nadia Kent, have reserves of strength inside of you you've not yet tapped. Add drive, talent, panache, and you can do anything you set your mind on. You don't need your mother's permission to soar."

Mention of her mother was quite enough for the adrenalin still sliding hot and molten through her veins to solidify like cooling candle wax. "Ryder—"

"Tell me you know it."

His eyes were no longer smiling. They were intense. Serious. Unrelenting. As if he believed in her. Not just her ability to dance. To do well despite her ex watching on. But *her.* And he wouldn't give up until she believed the same.

"I know it." And like a flash of white-hot light bursting inside her, illuminating the shiny new places inside her she'd only just begun to feel, she did. In fact in that moment she felt pretty much invincible.

Pure and unadulterated instinct taking her over, Nadia lifted up onto her toes, slid her hands over his big shoulders and kissed him. Soft at the start. Appreciating every lick of heat building in its wake. And when his hand moved to her breast, kneading, running a thumb over the centre, it ached. She ached. Every last bit of her inside and out, filled with such sweet pain she could barely stand it—

A car zoomed past, flushing them with a burst of hot air, and a beeping horn that echoed off into the distance. Still, they were slow to pull apart, and when Nadia leant her forehead against Ryder's shoulder the erratic beat of his heart more than matched her own.

"Lunch?" Ryder asked, his voice coarse.

"Sounds like a plan."

When Ryder dropped Nadia home late that evening, he helped her from the car once more. And once again made a meal of her self-control, the cold metal of the car at her back doing nothing to dampen the heat of the man kissing her senseless.

But after the events of the day—the news, revelations, and realisations—she was exhausted, emotionally and mentally wrung out. The thought of putting one foot in front of the other to get to her door was enough to make her whimper. So she pressed a hand to his chest. "Ryder, wait."

When he growled in frustration, she bit her lip so hard it bruised. She swiped her tongue over the spot, then said, "I've been thinking, and I need to cool things between now and the audition."

Hard, and hot, and breathing heavy, Ryder didn't move for a long while. When he did it was to curl away from her and lean back against the car, where he crossed his arms and looked out into the night.

"Like a football player," she explained, turning to face him, the cold of the car now seeping into her skin. "No sex before a big match. I'm going to need all the reserves of stamina I can muster. You understand, right?"

It shouldn't have been so hard. They both knew that with the audition looming, and Sam's wedding right on its heels, their places in one another's lives would lose traction and wind up. That time apart would all too soon be a final goodbye. And yet Nadia held her breath as she waited for his response.

"Yeah," he said, running his hand through his hair, before piercing her with a dark glance. "I understand."

Then casual as you please he ambled back to his side of the car, leaving Nadia to feel horribly bereft. Even though he'd given her exactly what she wanted. What she *needed*. Heck, he was the one who'd relit the fire under her with all that "you don't need your mother's permission" nonsense!

Desire, and exhaustion, and a goodly head of inner steam giving her a second wind, Nadia jogged across the cracked pavement leading to the heavily barred door below her apartment, and jabbed the key in the rusty lock.

"Nadia."

She turned to find him watching her over the car. His face in near darkness.

"Break a leg," he said, his words carrying a level of intensity that made her skin tighten all over at the thought he might not be wishing it in the spirit in which it ought to have been meant.

Nevertheless she said, "Thanks, Ryder."

Then without looking back she jogged up the skinny steps leading to her first-floor apartment, and went straight into her bedroom, and to the drawer where she kept her choreography notes.

She spent the next few hours staring at them, poring over them, tweaking them. Imagining herself going through the motions until she was sure the routine was the best thing she'd ever created. Because despite her exhaustion, her head was clear. Clear of the muddy conflicts and doubts and strangled hopes that had suffocated her efforts for as long as she could remember. And in the clarity she knew. She was ready. More ready than she'd ever been. To dance. For her. Just her.

Nadia ducked out of the train at Richmond Station.

Turning the collar of her light jacket against the shimmer of summer rain, she made her way along the platform, down the ramp and out onto the street leading to her apartment, where the malodorous scents of Laundromats, and student accommodation, and a million different kinds of international cuisine fought one another on the hot hazy air.

Adrenalin sent wings to her feet and she found herself doing her best *Singing in the Rain* all along the edge of the footpath, her feet feeling as if they barely touched the ground as the audition she'd just left played over and over in her head.

Not so much the moves; truth was she could barely remember a moment of the actual routine. It was the conversation afterwards that was still blowing her mind. Not only that the producers had been so lovely, so welcoming, so honestly thrilled to see her, but how they'd raved at her transformation.

Her technical perfection, they'd gushed, had been supercharged by some new raw emotion. A new-found vulnerability had added layers to her performance. A breakthrough, they'd said. Goose bumps had been mentioned. One woman claimed that with that final tool in her arsenal she was unstoppable. With that ringing in her head, who the hell cared that her stupid ex had barely looked her in the eye?

Seeing him had been *less* than she'd expected. Less hurtful. Less embarrassing. Maybe because she understood his part in the debacle, maybe because she'd recently begun to understand her own. Could she work with him if she got the gig? Hell, yeah. Could he work with her? That was his problem.

Needing to share this feeling before she burst, she pulled out her phone, opened her contacts list and there her thumb hovered. She wanted her friends in Vegas to know—they'd be cheering for her. Her reasons for wanting her mother to know were thorny and complicated. And yet there was only one person she truly wanted to tell, one person who would understand the layers of pride and relief and fear and excitement it had taken to dance on her own terms…

"Hey, Ginger Rogers," a deep voice called out.

Stopping short with one foot wavering in the air, she grabbed a lamppost to steady herself and held on tight. For there was Ryder, outside her apartment, leaning against his beautiful car in a pose that was as familiar to her as the man himself.

"Gene Kelly, actually," she said, her voice breathless, pocketing the phone with his number still on the screen.

It had been days since she'd seen him—since the driving lesson with the life lesson thrown in. It felt like weeks.

Pushing away from the shiny black hull of his car, he

came to her. A tall, dark presence who somehow still made her feel so light. "What's up?"

"You tell me. How did the audition go?"

"Seriously?" she blurted, fatally rapt that he'd remembered the time, the date, everything. She couldn't remember another time in her life when anyone cared enough to ask, at least not someone not competing against her for a part.

Then Ryder was there, his hands sliding around her waist, and she let go of the slippery post to hold his elbows. Tight. The familiar scent of him mingled with the rain in the air and she breathed it in deep. The heat of him coursed through her and her pulse thrummed right down deep.

"So?" he asked.

"Hmm?"

"The audition?"

"Right. Of course. It was…fabulous. I didn't want it to end. And they liked it. And me. And…well, that about covers it!"

His eyes roved over her face as she spoke, such intensity, such desire she near lost her train of thought. Then, eyes on hers, he slid a hand over her hair, coming up with a damp tendril. He wrapped it around a finger and tugged. "And the ex?"

Her skin, already feeling a size too small, zinged from his touch. "Still a douche."

He laughed, the deep sound rumbling through her, coiling the tension inside her tighter still. "And to think I'd been worried the guy'd take one look at you and fall to his knees and beg to have you back."

He'd been worried? Nadia felt so light-headed at the thought she figured she was way too low on electrolytes. But first she slid her hands up Ryder's big arms, over his strong shoulders, and she said, "He could beg all he likes. He's never getting me back."

He lifted his chin in acquiescence. "Good… For you,"

he added as an afterthought. "So how's your stamina, now the big match is over?"

That brought a grin to Nadia's face as she lifted onto her toes and pressed her mouth to his. The touch of their lips was gentle, tender even, as if they were relearning one another after their time apart. So tender her heart felt as if it was beating in her belly, emotion tightened the back of her throat, and she was pretty sure she'd begun to tremble.

Feelings tumbling through her like a waterfall over a craggy rock wall, Nadia tipped so high onto her toes she was practically *en pointe*. Then, though she wouldn't have thought it possible, when he held a soft hand at the back of her head the kiss grew deeper, more connected, and infinitely more precious.

Was it raining harder? Who knew? Who cared?

Wanting more, craving all, needing relief from the knots of pleasure twisting in her belly, she opened her mouth and Ryder took complete advantage. His tongue slid against hers, slowly, gently, but with absolute intent. When his tongue slid cruelly away, her teeth sank into his bottom lip in retribution, hard enough he hissed in a sharp breath.

Nadia stilled, while the heat continued to pour through her. Then with a groan Ryder swept his mouth over hers, enveloped her in his strong arms and kissed her till she saw stars.

Relearning done. This they knew how to do.

Her hands were beneath his jacket, sliding up the long flat muscles of his back, which twitched beautifully at her touch. Then with something akin to a roar he lifted her into his arms. She let out a loud *whoop* of surprise and held on tight—her arms around his neck, her legs around his waist.

"Keys?" he demanded.

"Back pocket."

His hand slid over her butt cheek until he found the necessary. Then, while she held on tight, laughing raggedly, breathlessly, by that stage, Ryder made his way to the door that led to her apartment and struggled manfully to unlock the thing, practically tearing the bars from their hinges as he let them inside.

And then Nadia's laughter disappeared as—compared to the bright shimmery light outside—they hit relative darkness. The naked globe at the top of the skinny stairs swept shadows across their faces, and the sounds of their intermingled breaths echoed off the old wallpapered walls.

Yet, even then there was no denying the hunger in Ryder's gaze.

Or the sudden dazzling wish in her heart that somehow it didn't have to end.

Nadia closed her eyes tight against the daze and kissed him. Out of sight of the rain and sky, away from prying eyes, just the two of them in the private contained space, the intensity of the kiss heightened. Deepened. Bringing with it an ache from where the wish had been born.

Nadia wriggled from Ryder's arms, and proceeded to tear her clothes from her body. Her frustration only built when it turned out the rain had stuck the cotton to her like glue.

"Oh, come on!" she cried out when her bra strap got caught on the strap of her top and held her like a straight-jacket.

Ryder lifted her bodily till she was a stair above. Then, face level with hers, he placed his big hands on her bare waist. Her muscles leapt at the skin-on-skin contact. His thumbs circled the edge of her ribs, his dark eyes following. She couldn't have been more glad that his eyes were anywhere but on hers, as there was no way she could hide the foolish feelings rushing about inside her, and no way she wanted him to see.

Fingers spanning her ribs, he rolled the layers of wet cotton up her body, over her breasts, and away. Her relieved sigh swept up the stairs, but was soon cut short as Ryder found her bare breast and took it in his mouth. His hot tongue swirled about the cool peak and her vision turned black.

With a groan that rocked the walls he arched her back as he took her other breast in his mouth. She trembled so much with the pleasure of it all she was very much afraid she might cry. She emptied her lungs on a long juddering breath and gave herself over to it. To him. To the absorption of his touch. The sexy shadowy darkness of the stairwell intensifying every shift, every sound, every slide of skin on skin.

When he lowered her to the stairs, she braced herself on her elbows. He tore her jeans down her thighs, taking her ballet flats with them, leaving her butt naked, while he was still fully clothed.

Before she even had a chance to rectify that, Ryder fell to his knees, pressed hers apart and took her in his mouth, his tongue, his hot lips, his not so steady breath driving her to an absolute craze until everything inside her spun out of control, and all she was, all she felt, was wave after wave of hot pleasure as it swept into a great aching that scooped her hollow. And just when she was sure she couldn't take it any more, the world stilled, lifted, swelled and splintered into a million points of light.

Body like rubber, mind complete pulp, her name came to her, the sound rolling over her skin like a caress, drawing her back to the present to find Ryder poised over her, his dark eyes burning into hers.

"Nadia," he said. That one word making her feel so much. Too much.

Closing her eyes against all it meant, she slid a hand behind his neck and pulled him to her. Vanishing into his kiss, his touch, his latent heat. This man who'd thought of her, waited for her, worried about her, and hadn't been able to keep his hands off her long enough to make it up one tiny flight of stairs…

She slid a leg along his to find his pants were gone. And with a smile she arched away from the stairs, wrapped her legs about the man and took him. Deep, hard. Her turn to cry out his name as he once again swept away every effort to keep him at emotional arm's length and once again sent her world crashing about her.

As they came back to earth Nadia held Ryder's head in the crook of her arm, breathing in when he breathed in, and staring at the paint peeling off the ceiling a half a floor above. As only now lying in the quiet with the big man's breaths easing over her skin, making her feel as if she were pure energy, barely bound, she knew where the "new raw emotion" the producers had raved about had come from. How she'd been able to "leave herself vulnerable" for the first time in her professional career.

But bar a malevolent miracle, or her ex having more influence than he deserved, she was going to Vegas. And soon. Her initial contract would be for six months, with an option to extend it out to two years if the show was a success. And it would be a success. Sky High was a phenomenon that showed no signs of waning.

And yet for a second, she let herself wonder…what if? What if she didn't get the job? What if they actually had a chance to take this thing for a spin and see where it might lead?

But a second was all it lasted. After Sam's wedding there would be no more dance lessons to keep them together. And the decision to remain so after that had been made before they'd even met. Because Ryder had been nothing but honest about his limitations as he saw them. About how his father's indiscriminate behaviour had burned him to the thought of for ever. And even while Sam claimed he held on tight to the things that mattered to him, despite the spark, despite the reverence in his touch and unquenched hunger in his eyes, despite the way he saw into the deep dark heart of her like nobody else she'd ever met, he'd never asked anything of her.

Not because she didn't matter; she just didn't matter *enough.*

And she'd been there, taken whatever scraps she was fed in the hopes of being loved. But something had shifted inside her these past few weeks. And she'd never *choose* to let herself not matter again.

Ryder lifted himself with a groan, his voice drugged, slow, deep. "Can you walk?"

"I've been known to."

They peeled themselves off the stairs, straightening as much clothing as possible.

She held out her hand, and after a moment Ryder took it, curling his big warm hand around hers before taking the stairs two at a time to lead the way. And when her heart thumped against her ribs at the feel of him, the sight of him, the knowledge that one day she'd wake up and know she'd never see him again, a little piece of her heart broke away from the whole.

And never, not once, for any other reason, did she wish harder that the Sky High gig would be through, and soon.

CHAPTER NINE

RYDER DIDN'T REALISE that he and Nadia had cruised into a kind of routine until the night it came to a halt.

The unions were threatening a city-wide walkout right when his latest project was at a crucial stage, and it had taken his team every ounce of charm to keep the worksite actually working when tension ran high enough to bring the whole thing crashing down on all their heads. But even as he'd headed back to his quiet apartment for a shower before he had to head to class, all he'd wanted to do was go to her.

Even considering the seismic scene on the stairs leading to her apartment, the thing he hadn't been able to get out of his mind was the volatile feeling that had erupted inside him when after few impossible days apart he'd seen her appear out of the mist, dancing in the rain.

He pressed the door open; the thought of catching her swinging from some dangerous contraption had him already harder than a beam.

He slowed when he saw she was already with someone—a skinny brunette he knew all too well. "Sam?"

"Hey, bro!" said Sam, a foot up on the barre, pretending to stretch like a knobbly-kneed ballerina.

"Hey, Ryder," Nadia called out, her back to him as she fiddled with the stereo.

Brow tightening, Ryder dumped his bag on the pink lounge. "What is she doing here?"

"Rehearsing," Nadia said, flicking him a glance that was far too perfunctory for his liking. "On the big day you'll be dancing with her, not me. So we thought the time had come for you to practise together."

Ryder would have bet his right elbow there was far more Nadia in that decision than *"we"*.

Sam ambled over to him, bumping him with a hip as she passed to grab a drink. "What she's too kind to say is I want to make sure you're not going to make a complete fool of yourself before I sign off on this thing."

Momentarily distracted by Sam's outfit—hot-pink leg warmers and an obscene green G-string leotard over shiny silver tights; she looked as if she'd stepped straight out of an eighties aerobics video—when he looked to Nadia there was gloom in her gaze. Though compared to his sister a disco ball would have seemed sinister.

Nadia clapped loudly, snapping him into reality. "Warm up!"

And Ryder gave himself a mental shake. Having a joint rehearsal was completely fair. And after an hour of the closest thing to living hell—dancing with his G-string-clad little sister—he'd have earned himself a trip to heaven.

Nadia took them through a few twists and bends and loosening exercises, then asked them to drop into a standing forward bend. He and Sam groaned and barely got their fingertips to their knees, while Nadia folded gracefully in half, the tips of her dark waves brushing the dusty floor.

"I've never been able to do that," Sam groaned.

Ryder squeezed his eyes shut when the thought that slipped into his mind was, *Poor Ben.*

"Practice, my sweet," said Nadia, not an ounce of strain in her voice as she lifted herself up straight. "After about the age of three being bendy only comes with practice."

Bendy, twisty, tricky, intoxicating, Ryder thought, catching Nadia's gaze before it slid past him and away. Okay, that time he knew he wasn't projecting. Definite shadows therein. And while that darkness did wicked things to his composure as it always did, he had to fight the urge to grab her by her bendy elbow and drag her to a quiet corner and ask her what the hell was going on.

Oblivious to the undercurrents, Sam groaned again as she pulled herself upright. "You've really been dancing since you were three?"

"Yep," said Nadia.

"So I'm a tad past it, then," said Sam. "Becoming a pro-dancer, that is."

Nadia laughed. "You've got a sudden hankering to go from standing ovations one day to in-your-face rejections the next?"

"I'd never looked at it that way. Harsh. How do you do it?"

"It's not so bad. I'm lucky I went in with my eyes wide open."

"Why's that?" Sam was bouncing from foot to foot by that stage, rolling her shoulders as if she were about to enter a prize fight, not practise a modified sway.

But Ryder only saw it from the corner of his eye as his focus was absorbed by Nadia, who looked as if she'd been jabbed with a cattle prod. And Ryder realised with a slow dawning that she must never have talked about this side of her life with Sam. Yet she had with him. The alpha wolf in him roared to life.

"Mum was a dancer," Nadia finally answered, staring at the remote as if it held the answer to life, the universe and everything. "And should therefore probably have been my cautionary tale. Alas, I caught the bug and that was the end for me."

With the alpha roar hampering his thought processes, Ryder slowly caught up. Something had definitely happened. In the hours since he'd seen her last, something had knocked her back into the darkness. Something that had made her bring Sam along as a shield. Ryder took a step her way, but whether by accident or design Sam bounced smack bang in front of him.

"Well, you're in the right city for it now," said Sam. "Melbourne is one of the most culturally rich cities in the world. There must be more work for a talent like you than you can bat away with a stick!"

Which was the moment Ryder realised *he'd* been the only oblivious one in the room.

His urge was now to drag *Sam* into a corner to ask her to explain herself. But Nadia's gaze had already zeroed in on his sister; his sensitive sister who didn't cope well with change, but who was also struggling with self-determination. Was *that* why she was doing her all to get him and Nadia together? Nadia who was in turn using Sam as a blockade.

And as the two women in his life stared one another down, hearts on their sleeves, his feet turned to lead. As for the first time in memory he didn't know what to do.

Nadia didn't have the same problem. She walked over to Sam, took her by the hips and spun her to face the windows; using one as a mirror, she pressed Sam's shoulders back and lifted her arms into a dance hold. "I'm going to miss you like crazy too, Sammy Sam. But I can't stay here. Even if I don't get the Sky High job, there'll be another. And it will be somewhere else other than here."

"Why?" Sam asked, tears springing into her eyes.

Nadia leant her chin on Sam's shoulder. "Because while this has been lovely, and wonderful, and curative, it's time for me to get back to my real life."

Sam's mouth twisted as she looked at Nadia's eyes in the reflection. Then Nadia gave her a squeezing hug from behind and said, "Okay?"

Which unbelievably made Sam laugh and say, "Okay."

While all Ryder could think was, *She's leaving. She's really leaving. And she's started saying goodbye.*

Nadia sat perched on the edge of the pink velvet chaise and simply breathed.

It had taken a good half-hour before things finally settled into the groove she'd been desperate for when she'd called Sam that afternoon and all but begged her to come. A conversation she'd had about fifteen minutes after getting off the phone with her mum.

Determination giving her wings, she'd called to tell her mother about the awesome audition. She'd couched it in wanting Claudia to know she might be leaving the country soon, in case she, you know, actually cared. When that had made little discernible impression on the woman Nadia had turned into a babbling idiot—*they loved me, they really loved me!* And it had only gone downhill from there.

Nadia dropped her head into her hands and groaned under her breath. She was a lost-effing-cause. She could dance without her mother's acceptance; Ryder had been right about that. But it seemed she still couldn't *live* without it.

Sky High or no Sky High, the only way she could see to cut herself off from the passive-aggressive abuse for good was to go away, far away, and this time to stay.

And no matter how appealing, how enticing the possibilities that had barreled through her after Ryder had come to her after the audition, all the glowing what-ifs in the world couldn't stand up to that one great truth.

Laughter spilled from the centre of the room, cutting through the dulcet sound of Norah Jones. Nadia followed the sound to where Sam was in Ryder's arms, their dark heads tilted towards one another. They laughed softly as they danced, Sam instructing, Ryder telling her to shut the hell up and let him lead, eyes mostly on one another's feet.

Not a subtle bone in that girl's body, Nadia thought, her heart giving a little squeeze. Sweet though, what she'd been trying to do. Bittersweet. As for her brother…

Nadia's breath lodged in her throat as Ryder's eyes found hers, and not for the first time. As he moved confidently through the steps, he couldn't seem to keep from looking her way. Every glance forcing her to add a new brick to the wall she was rebuilding around her heart. Because he'd taken a piece of it the other day, turning up after her audition as he had.

But she couldn't hope to really make the very most of this next phase of her life clinging to the previous. She knew better than anyone.

The song ended and Ryder twirled Sam out to the end of one hand before twirling her back again, Sam's adorable laughter filling the studio till it tinkled off the windows. One of the bricks around her heart crumbled and fell.

When Ryder wrapped his arms around his little sister and dropped a kiss atop her head, it took everything Nadia had not to crumble completely at the tenderness of it all. The adoration. Intimate, private, true. It was like a foreign language to Nadia, and yet in that moment she felt a funny flicker of comprehension. As if she just needed to tilt herself on the right angle and she'd understand it all.

And then, when Ryder's gaze once more landed on hers, and he smiled just for her, like a flash bomb blooming from the centre of her heart and all the way out to her extremities, she understood all too well. She did everything in her power to contain the ominous surge, employing every formidable muscle, every bullet-proof nerve, every form of self-protection she had in her potent arsenal.

They didn't make a dent. The light of her tender feelings for Ryder filled her till it all but lifted her from the chair.

Her heart continued to beat. Her lungs continued to breathe. Yet she knew everything had changed. Only with the familiar dull ache of her messy conversation with her mother still riding her, and with no example of what the hell to do about these wholly new feelings flinging about inside her, all she could do was rewrap herself in the scattered remains of her fortitude, and hold on tight.

Her throat felt raw when she called out, "That's a wrap, kids."

"But we have ten more minutes!" said Sam, the adrenalin of the dance still pouring through her.

"I do believe Miss Nadia intends for us to quit while we're all ahead."

Nadia flinched as Ryder's deep sonorous voice slid inside her as if he had some kind of inside track. Some door only he knew how to open. She wished she could just shut it down, but she hadn't a clue where the opening was.

"That's right, kid!" she said, standing and wrapping an arm about Sam's shoulders. "You done good. So scat."

With a sigh, and a twirl, Sam gathered her things, gave Nadia a kiss on the cheek, informed them Ben had been waiting in the car below the whole time, then disappeared out the door, leaving Nadia alone with Ryder after all.

"Are you going to tell me what happened?" Ryder said, cutting to the point.

"You're ready, that's what," she said, avoiding eye contact as she pretended to tidy sheets of piano music that hadn't been looked at in decades. "Now I can safely send you two out onto that dance floor and not be mortified to put my name to it."

"That's not what I mean and you know it. You've had news?"

News? The auditions. Right.

She tensed when she felt him move in behind her. And when Ryder's hand landed on her waist the light inside her shone so bright it was blinding. It took everything she had not to lean into all that strength and warmth. Instead she turned out of his grasp, and held onto the bookshelf behind her for support. “No news. Not for a few days, I’d say. Maybe longer.”

Ryder’s hot eyes landed on her mouth, and her brain waves skittered out of control. Only now she’d somehow lost the ability to bring them back to earth.

“I’d wondered,” he said, frowning even as his eyes darkened. “Considering you’ve been acting like a cat on a hot tin roof since I arrived.”

She had? Oh, right. Her mum. The light inside her dimmed a fraction, which should have been welcome, but instead she fisted her hands at her side and tried to press her mother out of her head. Out of her damn heart. The reason Nadia wasn’t coping with the feelings skittering about inside her like a normal person was because of *her* in the first place.

“Everything else okay?”

She shook her head. Nodded. Opened her mouth to tell him about the call, knowing this man of all men would understand better than anyone.

But it wasn’t his concern. Could never be.

She took a deep breath and looked him in the eye. “Everything’s hunky-dory.”

Smart guy, he clearly didn’t believe her. But for whatever reason he didn’t press. Instead he said, “Prove it. Let go of the damn shelf, woman, and come here.”

Despite the emotional roller coaster going off the rails inside her, Nadia’s mouth twitched into a smile. And following her wicked feet and anaemic heart, she went to him, but at the last she pressed her hand against his chest, as if keeping their hearts apart was her last stand.

“You may have led Sam with some aplomb back there, Ryder, but I’ll have you know I’m still the boss in this room.”

One dark eyebrow slid up his forehead. “You just go on

thinking that, Miss Nadia," he said, his voice gruff as he pressed her back against the shelves, dust and papers raining down upon their heads. "If it helps you sleep at night."

Her heart kicked like a wild thing as his eyes dropped back to her mouth, eyes filled with desire and defiance, and she knew that she wouldn't be sleeping much that night, if at all.

It's sex. Just sex. Delicious, exquisite, earth-moving sex. He's been your port in a storm. A little night comfort in a far-off land. Nothing new there; that's totally your MO.

Yeah, she thought, *you just keep telling yourself that*, as his mouth descended on hers, sensation took over and all thought fled.

Ryder ran a hand over his neck. It ached from too many hours at the computer in his office atop a giant Collins Street edifice.

And yet it hadn't been a skyscraper keeping him locked to his chair. It had been sketch after sketch of a large space filled with arched windows and high beams and old wooden floors. A building with a broken lift, lights that appeared on the verge of burning the whole place down. With strips of red silk floating from one discreet corner.

He'd been thinking about the place so much of late, to the detriment of his real work. His only option as he saw it was to get the thing out of his head. The sheaths of paper curled up on the carpet beside his shoes proved it hadn't worked.

Ryder stood, stretched his arms over his head, and felt his spine crick and crack. Then, remembering the posture Nadia had shown him, pressed his feet into the floor from his hips down, and pulled himself as tall as possible from his hips up, as if his body were squashed between two panes of glass… His muscles sang with the relief and release of it, until he caught sight of how ridiculous he looked in the window.

He could have kissed his mobile when it rang.

"Hey, kiddo," he said, after seeing Sam's number on the display, "just the distraction I needed."

"We got married!" her crackly voice exclaimed.

"Say again?" Ryder stuck his finger in his other ear and headed to the window to make sure he had the best reception possible. Because she could not possibly have just said—

"We eloped! I am now officially Mrs Ben Johnson!"

"It sure as hell sounded like you just said that you eloped."

A pause, then, "That's because I did. I told Ben everything. About Dad, and the other wives, and the panic attacks. And he was a rock, Ryder. He was beautiful, and perfect, and strong, and wonderful. And we're in Las Vegas right now. And it's gorgeous. We flew in at night and the lights—"

But Ryder hadn't heard much past *Vegas*. The bloody place was fast turning out to be his arch enemy. "Did Nadia put you up to it?"

After a long pause, Sam shot back, "In what possible way?" her voice tight. When he was the only one with any right to be pissed.

"She's from Vegas. And don't try to say you didn't know."

"She's not from here. She's *from* there."

"Well, she's moving back there any day now." He knew he was pulling at straws, but he was struggling to get his head around it all.

"Oh." Sam's suddenly soft voice broke through. "Has she heard when?"

She hadn't. Not when he'd left her soft and warm and naked in her bed at five that morning. When he'd actually toyed with the thought of doing the walk of shame into work in the same suit and tie he'd worn the day before, just to get another hour in her arms.

"That's not the point," he growled. "What the hell possessed you guys?"

"It had all just spun so far out of control, Ryder. It was meant to have been small, just us and Ben's family, and you giving me away. And then all that stuff happened with Dad, and on Ben's side a fight had erupted over what flavour cake might offend Great-Auntie Wallace. In the end we realised we just wanted to look one another in the eye and say, *It's you. You're it. You're the one who makes my heart race and my bed warm and I'll take that for ever, thank you very much.*"

Ryder closed his eyes and rubbed his thumb and forefinger over the bridge of his nose. What the hell could he possibly say to that? "And Vegas was your only option?"

"It was quickest," she said, and he could all but hear her grin. "A sixty-dollar licence and a five-minute ceremony and you're done. You should have seen the line-up at the courthouse. Picture women in full bridal regalia, their limos waiting at the kerb. Men in Elvis wigs, their luggage at their feet as they'd come straight from the airport."

Picturing it wasn't helping. "I just wish…" He wished what? That he could go back to the way things were when he was her everything, and she was his, and his life was laid out ahead of him like a long dark tunnel of more of the same? "I just wish I'd been there to see it."

"I know." He heard the wobble in her voice, before she took a great big sniff. "But then we had that dance, you and I. That perfect, lovely dance at Nadia's. *That* was our dance, Ryder. Not in front of a million people I barely know. Not looking over our shoulders waiting for Dad to ruin everything. That night at Nadia's studio—you gave me away."

His thoughts slipped back to that conversation in his car a few weeks back when she'd "set him free". And he knew then why it had felt like a false victory—it had never been about Sam setting him free; he was the one who needed to let *her* go. And that night in the dance studio, watching Sam and Nadia go head to head, he'd not only given her her first real taste of independence, he'd taken his first step into his own.

"Yeah," he said. "I did."

"Lucky for you," said Sam, "the cabana boy wants to be a cinematographer so he took the video for us."

"Lucky me."

And then his sister was babbling about the lights and the casinos and that you could sit in the Keno bar all night, play a game an hour and get as many free Long Island iced teas as you wanted.

"You sound happy, Sam."

Her breath shook. "So, so happy."

"Love you, kiddo," Ryder said before he bloody well joined her.

"Love you more."

And then she was gone. Leaving Ryder alone in his big office, with the moonlight and etchings his only companions.

He looked out at the view over the city, glancing over the number of significant new buildings he'd had a hand in creating. His legacy. And he waited for…something. A feeling of satisfaction. Or pride. Even relief that for the first time in more than half his life he had only himself to consider.

But no matter how long he stood there, he didn't feel a damn thing.

Because the honest truth was, the only decision hanging in the balance in his life wasn't up to him. It was in the hands of a bunch of tights-wearing strangers on the other side of the planet. And there was not a damn thing he could do about it.

CHAPTER TEN

LONG SHADOWS SLICED through the golden glow of the street below as Nadia left the studio in daylight for the first time on a Tuesday in over two months.

She knew Ryder wouldn't be there leaning against his big black car. Dance lessons were over; Sam's crazy, wonderful elopement a couple of days earlier had put paid to that. Yet the empty street tugged painfully at her stomach.

She jogged down the steps and headed towards her spartan rooms where everything was so temporary. So quiet. All those hours ahead of her in which to think.

She could have stayed and rehearsed, but she just didn't have the urge. And with Sam and Ben away she couldn't call on them to go out dancing to shake off the odd sense that she was in limbo. Waiting. As if the other shoe were out there, dangling above her and about to drop right on her head.

She turned up the collar of her light jacket, shoved her hands into the pockets and turned the corner, picking up the pace as a light drizzle filled the air, taking the edge off the heat as the longest, hottest summer of her life drew to a close.

But in spite of how far she walked, the tension still rode her, made her muscles tight, her stomach hard, her head jittery. Another day of not knowing what was around the corner for her—much less another ten—and she'd be off her nut.

And there was only one way she could think to ease the pressure that had been building inside her for days. *Ryder.* She walked faster instead. Because she couldn't go there. Especially not after she'd taken that swan dive into fairy-land the other night.

In retrospect she put the whole thing down to a mini emotional breakdown. Still roiling from the aloofness of her mum's phone call, and then mixing in Sam's supreme happiness and the big man's total tenderness, as well as the realisation her time in Melbourne was coming to an end—it had all whirled into some great vortex of syrupy sentiment.

Which meant that Sam's elopement could *not* have come at a better time. If they wanted a neat and tidy end to what had been morphing into a more complicated affair than either of them had signed up for, they'd been handed it on a platter.

Unfortunately her body didn't agree. Turned out she couldn't walk fast enough to get away from thoughts of his hot touch, his strong hands, his devastating mouth.

A cab pulled up at the kerb ahead, letting out a passenger. Her feet stalled to a halt, her knees twitching, her teeth clamping down on her lip.

Then before she knew it she was running up to the driver, asking if he was free to do a drop-off in Brighton, and was in the back seat and away. It felt like less than a minute before she was out of the cab and walking up to Ryder's stunning split-level near the beach.

Her hair was damp from the rain. Goose bumps tightened her skin to the point of pain. Her heart knocked hard and heavy against her ribs, opening them up with each beat until she felt as if she were completely exposed. Then, as if she were a magnet and Ryder the centre of the earth, she lifted a hand and knocked.

Blood pumping so hard she could barely hear the traffic and waves and thrash of the wind as the drizzle whipped up into a late summer storm, Nadia waited. The ground tilting out from under her as she realised he might not even be home. And worse, if he was, the second he opened the door and saw her there, he'd know—

"Nadia?" Ryder said, surprise lighting his voice as he did just that.

He was decked out in old jeans that had clearly seen a worksite or two and a black shirt untucked with the sleeves rolled up. His hair was mussed and his jaw unshaven. And he looked so beautiful, so strong, so vital Nadia's thumping heart leapt right into her throat and stayed there.

Her mouth opened but nothing came out. What could she possibly say? The truth? That her last few days were a fog? That her feet had just brought her there? That her mini emotional breakdown was still very much in force? Either that or she was falling in love for the first time in her life and that she was terrified she'd spend the rest of her life aching without him.

But she'd never had a relationship that didn't end. Had never had anyone in her life who'd stuck around. Not when she'd asked, not when she'd enticed. Not when she'd out and out begged.

Give a damn and they'll eat you alive.

Which was how she summoned the remaining echoes of a lifetime of feigned ambivalence, ducked a hip against the doorjamb and looked up at him beneath her lashes. "It's Tuesday night. And for the first time in for ever I have no plans. You?"

He stood there, a wall of strength and quiet, saying nothing. And a flood of mortification flowed thick and fast through her. Oh, God, she was really alone in this, wasn't she? The only one feeling at a loss. Like every other time she'd dared to reach out to someone in her life. She took a step backward—

Ryder's hand clamped over her wrist, and he pulled her to him, and his lips were on hers, her hands in his hair, not an ounce of dying daylight between them as he walked her inside.

He slammed the door shut with his foot before he was all over her again. Ridding her of her bag, her scarf, her jacket. Flicking her hair out of the way to get to her neck.

She leant into him with a sigh, sensation pummelling her; her hair was everywhere, her skin already slicked with sweat. Too much feeling shooting through her to slow it down before it consumed her.

Not that Ryder gave her a chance. With a growl he found a wall and pressed her up against it. And their clothes were gone, skin on skin, his heat filling her up, the light inside her so bright it spilled over in her sighs, her moans, the damp gathering at the corners of her eyes.

And then he was inside her and Nadia spiralled so far down the rabbit hole there was nothing but the deepest delectation and absolute relief.

Ryder held the mobile phone tight in his hand, not sure how long he'd been sitting up in his bed staring at the screen. Seconds probably, considering it had yet to hibernate to black, and yet it felt like for ever.

"Ryder?" Nadia's sleepy voice murmured from beside him, just before she snuggled her face into his hip, her arm curling possessively about his thigh. "Was that my phone?"

Ryder gripped the thing a moment longer, stalling, stretching time, before he accepted time had run out. "It rang. I didn't get to it in time."

Nadia dragged herself to sitting, bringing his sheet with her. Knees to her chest, she swept the messy mass of her hair from a face soft with sleep and swiped a thumb over the screen. She got halfway through a yawn before she saw the name that had stopped his heart.

Wide awake now, her eyes shot to his. Even in the soft wash of moonlight he saw how big they were. And how damned excited. “I was expecting an email. They said they’d email.” She swept her hair from her eyes again; this time her movements were quick, breathless. “I’m sorry. I have to—”

“Go ahead,” he said, leaning back against his pillow with his arms propped behind his head, like a man with not a care in the world. When truthfully, his insides were coiled so tight that his lungs struggled to fill.

She spun away from him, her toes dropped to the floor, and she curled over her phone with both hands as if it were something precious. Within seconds her voice hummed into the thing. “Sorry, Bob, I was asleep.” Laughter, then, “No, that’s fine. But only because it’s you.” Then came a series of quiet *mmm-hmms*.

Ryder closed his eyes and, for the first time since he found a thirteen-year-old Sam in the midst of her first panic attack frozen to the point of near catatonia, he prayed.

When he realised what he was praying for, his eyes snapped open. And his blood ran cold.

Nadia slowly hung up the phone and held it in her lap, her naked back curved towards him, her dark waves spilling over the unearthly pale skin, her scent of her all over his sheets, all over his skin.

And he knew.

Strike that. He’d known from the moment she’d walked towards him so dark and lush and tempting that any part she played in his life would be transitory, titanic, fatal.

“When?” he asked.

She turned so one leg was hooked onto the bed, and glanced quickly over her shoulder before turning back to the phone, and in that glance he saw that any excitement that might have been there was now lost beneath the quicksilver mess of emotion shimmering across her face. "Next weekend. No, *this* one. Bob's emailing flight details right now."

Ryder somehow nodded, even while he was blistering on the inside from the effort not to hold her, touch her, lose himself in her every last moment they had together. But mostly from the effort not to make good on his prayer and do whatever it took to make her stay.

Because it was going to be brutal. Hell, if she hadn't come to him that night, by five minutes to ten he'd have been ripping her door off its hinges. Like some seductive vapour she'd invaded his thoughts, his needs, his life. At times when they were apart he could have sworn he could feel her energy flowing through him as if she'd seeped into his very marrow.

And considering her history, he had no doubt he could chisel that fissure of hesitation into full-blown uncertainty. A kiss just below her ear, a thumb run softly along her jaw, a stroke of her inner thigh and he could make her his. But for how long? Until another opportunity like this came along? Until things naturally simmered down? Until disillusion leached in, restlessness took hold, and he realised he'd had enough?

He knew how badly she wanted the job, how much of her own self-worth was wrapped in whether or not she had it in her to succeed on her own, how much healthier it would be if she got as far away as possible from the insidious destructive influence of her mother, and yet he'd yearned for her to fail. Just so he could keep her close.

If he'd ever harboured any small hope that he might one day be able to love a woman in a more honest way than his own father ever had, that doubt had just been pulverised.

He was a selfish bastard. Which was his problem, not hers. His hit to take.

As he saw it he had one chance at redemption. He had to let her go. And he had to do so in a way that meant she'd never look back.

"You appear a little shell-shocked, Miss Nadia."

In profile her forehead scrunched into a frown. "Probably because I am."

"I thought you'd be bouncing off the walls. Literally." He said it with a smile that felt as if it had been cut into his face.

Then she turned to him, her eyes wide, her lips pursed, her expression…lost. "What if I'm not ready? What if I'm kidding myself? What if it's not what I really want? What if I've been too busy running towards what I think I should want to see that what I really want is something else—something right under my nose?"

Dammit. Nadia. Sweetheart.

Ryder lifted off the pillow and slid a hand up her spine before it curled around the back of her neck. Her soft skin and sleepy warmth carved a hollow in his chest. "You forget, I've seen you spinning circles in the sky. Of all the people I've met in my life, you are the one who's had the most manifest purpose. That show is what you were born to do."

"You think?"

"I know."

"Ryder," she said, pulling away. Her eyes glistened, swarming with emotion he understood more than he let himself dwell on. What had happened between them might be real, it might feel rich and thick and true, but he couldn't promise it would last. And he wouldn't risk hurting her simply for the chance to find out.

"I *know*," he said, holding her gaze until she breathed out, and belief poured back into her dark, soulful eyes.

And then she leant into him. Snuggling into his touch. Trusting and soft and small. *Adorable*, he thought. And between breathing out and breathing in again, Ryder felt something inside him split right in half, the pain of it cracking through him like a gunshot.

But she didn't need to know the arguments his conscience and his ego were battling out inside him. What she needed was sleep. And to feel damn proud of herself. So he laid her down, and rolled her into his arms, wrapping her up until her head fitted just under his chin and her breath shifted against his chest.

He lay there, all night, staring at the phone still clutched in her hand, telling himself he'd done the right thing.

When Nadia woke up the next morning, Ryder was gone.

She reached out for him to find his side of the bed empty and cold and on his pillow a note. A note and an apple.

For the road, the note read.

And the lump that had formed in her throat the moment she'd seen the Sky High producer's name on her phone dislodged itself and the tears that had gathered behind it poured from her eyes like a damn waterfall.

Because she loved the idiot.

Up and down, through and through. She'd known it with absolute certainty the moment Bob had told her she was in. She should have felt elated, over the moon, vindicated, relieved. Instead all she'd felt was a keening sadness whistling through a hole in her heart.

Even while she'd seen in his eyes that he felt…something, if not love then a definite desire to keep her close, he'd congratulated her, wished her luck, and held her with such tenderness she'd slept like a log. And woken not to the man who'd misappropriated her heart, but a damn apple, and a note that as good as warned her not to let the door hit her on the backside on the way out.

Was that it? Good luck and thanks for all the sex? Because he simply didn't care, or because he cared too much for some drawn-out farewell?

She couldn't think surrounded by his heat, his scent, the bachelor pad to end all bachelor pads. She had to get out of his bed. She swiped her palms over her damp cheeks, and then tried to untwist herself from the sheets, but they fought back. By the time she'd yanked herself free she tumbled out of bed and onto the floor with a thump.

And there she lay, breathing heavily, looking up at the ceiling as she had the first night she met him. Only this time it wasn't the ceiling of her lonely little flat. And this time she wasn't lost, wasn't filled with hope that she might one day get her act together. This time all her dreams had come true.

All the dreams she'd ever had until she met him.

With a groan she pulled herself upright, wincing at the bruises on her backside, which would be black and blue by the time she got to Vegas in a few days. *A few days.* That was all the time she had to tie up the loose threads of the life she'd built. And the more she thought about it, the more threads there were. So many unexpected goodbyes.

"Then you'd better get cracking," she said, the croak less convincing than she'd hoped.

She was dressed and out of the door within minutes. She only held onto the doorknob a moment. Okay, a few moments. But she had to be sure this time, certain of what she was walking away from.

"Love," she said out loud, the word picked up by the sea breeze and carried away on the wind. For the first time in her life, love.

But Sky High was what she wanted. It *was*. It had better be, because it would be her whole life now. Her days and her nights. Her blood and her sweat. Her bruised bones and her tweaked tendons. And as for her inflamed heart?

With a growl she pushed away from the door and jogged down the steps to the footpath.

She'd had her heart crushed a thousand times in her

life and survived. So long as she had dance, she'd survive Ryder Fitzgerald too.

With that mantra on a loop inside her head as she walked down the beach road towards her tram stop, Nadia didn't look back.

CHAPTER ELEVEN

MELBOURNE PUT ON A most beautiful day. After the weeks of rain and overcast skies the heavens were clear, only a few puffy white clouds marring their perfection. Down on the peninsular the air was more fresh, the salty breeze a reminder how close Ryder was to the sea.

With a plane taking Nadia away that day, Ryder hadn't trusted himself not to bite the head off some poor contractor on site, so he'd taken a road trip south until he found himself on a very different kind of site, the kind he hadn't set foot on in years.

Before him loomed a big old house. It listed away from a dangerously pitched cliff face as a result of years of buffeting winds and was now held in place by carefully built scaffolding. Around the property lay palettes of stained glass, piles of old wood, and mounds of new bricks peeking out from beneath paint-speckled tarps.

And just like that his palms itched with the memory of having an actual hammer in his grip, wood and nail meeting with a satisfying jar. It was a memory of his summer days learning the trade in places like this, and of watching his mother grin as she knocked together creations of her own. Either way it felt…good. And after the oblivion of the past few days he'd take all the therapy he could get.

"Ryder!" a familiar voice called out, and he turned to find Tom Campbell bearing down on him.

It had been over a decade since he'd last worked for the guy, acting as labourer's apprentice down in Portsea in his determination to pay his own way through college. Even with the salt-and-pepper hair and deeper crinkles around his eyes, he looked more robust than ever.

"You look ridiculously healthy," Ryder said, shaking his hand. "Sea air? Honest work? Botox?"

"Try the love of a good woman."

Right, shouldn't have asked. "Show me what you're up to."

With a grin of pure delight, Tom distracted Ryder beautifully by taking him through his latest house project, a renovation job he didn't need for the guy was loaded, but one he did for the thrill of bringing old glory back to life.

And as Ryder took in the beautiful mouldings, the original stone fireplace now peeking through a hole in the horrendously wallpapered plasterboard, of all the spots he could have gone in an effort to find his feet again, this was the place. He felt more grounded here than he had in a long time. More stimulated by the random house than any building he'd produced from scratch. Because this was what he'd gone into architecture *for.*

Uncovering the inherent beauty in lost things.

And the years began to tumble in on him, brick by brick, till he was breathing in the dust of his memories, the ache of that long ago day when, covered in sweat and grime and speckles of paint, he'd had the future of his dreams in sight only to have his father corrupt it with his cruel words and snatch it right away.

Only from the outside looking in he realised that it wasn't that simple. Fitz had been his usual ruinous self—but so full of spit and fire and hostility the decision to quit had been Ryder's own. His father had altered the course of his life because Ryder had let him.

The irony hit like a roundhouse kick to the solar plexus.

Like that long ago day, he'd let the bastard do it again. And this time he hadn't even been in the same room.

Needing air, space, perspective, Ryder excused himself and steered himself back outside. And the moment he stepped into the sunshine he saw it—a plane soaring overhead. Who knew where it was headed? Probably Sydney, or Brisbane. Outer Mongolia for all he knew. The chances it was heading to Las Vegas were slim to none. And yet he didn't look away. He couldn't. He watched, lungs tight, skin tingling, feet pressing hard into the rocky ground until the plane was well out of sight and he could tell himself Nadia was gone. Really gone.

He'd lost her. Hell, he'd miss her. He tried telling himself he'd done the right thing. The benevolent thing. That nothing lasted for ever. Not relationships. Not old houses built on windy bluffs. Not even skyscrapers built of the strongest materials known to man.

Except for the fact that he hadn't lost Nadia, he'd *let her go.*

And she'd let him let her go because she'd been let down so many times in her life it was all she knew how to do.

Dammit, thought Ryder, closing his eyes tight, blocking out the light as he tried to capture any one of the fragile threads of thought shifting through his head. That somewhere there was an answer. A different answer. The real answer. *His* answer.

Something about Sam. His little sister finally putting her foot down and living her life on her terms. Because of Ben. Because the kid's love meant more to her than their father's betrayals.

And then—lungs filled with the heady scents of paint stripper and putty, of wood varnish and plaster dust, of imagination, dedication, and optimism—he caught it.

He loved Nadia.

He *loved* her with a depth he couldn't see to the bottom of. And, try as he might, he couldn't imagine a time when he wouldn't feel the same way. Because Nadia wasn't some girl he was trying to forget for her own good. She was *his* girl. His equal, his foil, his conscience, his advocate. His partner.

Ryder had believed it was in his genes that he'd never be able to love that way, and time had never proven him wrong. But the truth was, he just hadn't known how until he met her. She'd filled his life, connected him deeper to himself than he'd ever been. And in that darkness, deep down inside, she flickered. She'd always flicker. His truth. His light. His love.

Ryder ran a hand through his hair and took a few steps right, then left. But he had no idea where he was meant to go. Only that he hoped it wasn't too late. That he hadn't martyred himself out of the best thing that had ever happened to him.

When it finally hit him where he was meant to be he called out his goodbyes to Tom and took off towards his car at a run.

Nadia leant her head against the window of the cab and watched the Las Vegas scenery flicker by—wide plots of vacant land populated by dry brown scrub and tumbleweed, huge outlet malls, wedding chapels, drug stores and casinos so big that the time away had made far smaller in her mind.

The years she'd looked out over Vegas' shimmery horizon every day felt like a lifetime ago. Her year in Melbourne was still far too significant. The memories too raw. The people left behind like anchors around her neck.

But seeing old friends, visiting old haunts, making new memories would take care of that. As would setting up her silks, getting back into the swing of the hoop and enduring the punishment of the rehearsal schedule. She would immerse herself so deeply in the dance that by the time she came blinking back out into the real world the permanent ache in the centre of her chest would have faded. Some of it at least. Oh, she hoped so.

And then Norah Jones came on the cab's radio.

Her mind filled with the memories of other car rides. Of Melbourne rain sliding down other windows, and down her back. Of dancing with a deep voice in her ear, a hot chest against her own as she swayed with no purpose other than to be near. Of sharp suits and shiny shoes. Of bare feet curled over hers in bed, a strong arm wrapped possessively over her naked waist—

"We're here, missy."

The taxi driver's twang snapped Nadia out of her reverie. She stared blankly at the guy, who grinned as he leant his arm on the back rest of his seat, no doubt mistaking her silence for awe.

"What's the plan?" he asked. "Gonna win big? Get yourself hitched?"

"I'm a dancer," she said, the words settling her some. "In the new Sky High show."

His eyebrows disappeared beneath a thatch of dyed black hair; the guy probably moonlighted as an Elvis impersonator. "Never seen a show, but my girlfriend can't get enough of them. Know what? I'll be sure to see yours, since I can say I met you and all."

Nadia paid out the fare. "Do. It'll blow your mind."

The driver shrugged, as if being local to this part of the world it'd take a hell of a lot more than a fancy dance show to surprise him.

Check-in papers in one hand, handle of her small wheelie case packed with her meagre worldly possessions in the other, Nadia looked up at the multicoloured façade of the structure that would be her home until she found herself a place. She would be sharing accommodation with a bunch of the other dancers, no doubt. Rehearsing all day. Partying all night. And when the show began it would be two shows a day, six days a week, for months on end. Her ankles killing her, her knees protesting, her hands worn till they resembled those of a woodchopper…

Her dream come true.

The double doors slid open and she was instantly hit with the sound of slot machines a level above. The carpet was a Harlequin pattern in a riot of eye-watering colour, the walls just as chaotic.

She joined the line at Reception behind a group on a girls' weekend, and another at a buck's party. She could all but see tomorrow's hangovers in their eager faces.

Better get used to it. They were the minutiae of her new life. Her people. Day trippers and weekenders. Honeymooners and gamblers. And a dance company of thick-skinned kids with hollow legs and a taste for danger. Transient and impulsive. Drawn to the bright lights and constant noise. Never wondering if they were really living the dream or simply blinded by fluorescent lights, endless buffets and not a second's down time to just think.

No shiny-faced Tiny Tots who thought her an honest to goodness fairy princess here.

No senior pole dancers who found more simple joy hooking a leg around a chair than most of her peers did successfully completing a triple-twist death drop.

No boss who remembered her birthday and gave her the day off, and gift certificates to get massages if she looked worn out.

No local markets where the stall owners knew her by name.

No Sam and Ben. Or the sweet crew of fun, crazy friends who actually cared about one another and would have laughed themselves silly at the very thought of competing against one another for anything.

Nadia breathed deep, held the suitcase handle tighter

again, and did her all to stop the next name from slipping into her mind. But there was no stopping it. No stopping him. There never had been. From the moment he'd waltzed into her studio, so magnificent and foreboding, it was as if her soul had said, *So there you are.*

But he wasn't there now. Not any more.

As it always did at such moments, her mother's voice seeped in knocking her to *get up, move on, stay tough.* And most of all not make the same mistake she had, in letting her future go up in smoke for some guy. Well, it had sunk in all right, because here she was, with the job of a lifetime in the palm of her hot little hand, while the guy she loved was thirteen thousand kilometres away.

It might as well have been a million, she thought, looking over her shoulder where the automatic doors slid open and closed to accommodate the constant stream of strangers. The angle showcased a handful of hotels down the strip, the peculiar golden sun of Nevada making them appear like a mirage, a fantasy that would dissolve into sand at the first strong wind.

"Welcome to the King's Court Hotel and Casino!"

Nadia flinched and turned back to Reception to find a woman in a red and navy jester's outfit with big silver bells tinkling on the tips of her crazy hat.

"Pray tell, what can I do you for, today?" When Nadia didn't answer, the receptionist waggled her fingers at the passport and papers in Nadia's hand. "Checking in?"

Nadia nodded, and handed over her work papers, unable to take her eyes from the bells. *Tinkle tinkle.*

"Oh, wonderful!" said the receptionist. *Tinkle tinkle.* "You're with the new show! I wish I could dance—two left feet though. Though I guess there's dance and there's what you lot do. I poked my head in on rehearsal the other day and…wow! You are so lucky, to have the ability to back up what you want to do with your life."

The woman's hat tinkled some more as the automatic doors again opened behind Nadia, bringing with them a gust of dry desert air that lifted the hairs on the back of her neck. When, after a pause, the receptionist's smile began to waver, Nadia realised she was still gripping her papers with one hand.

Because as if the blast of air had dumped a flurry of pixie dust from one of the magic shows down the strip onto Nadia's head, her mind emptied till it was left with the receptionist's perky voice saying, *You are so lucky, to have the ability to back up what you want to do with your life.*

She absolutely had the ability to back up what she wanted to do with her life, and she always had, because she *hadn't* made the same mistake her mother had.

Her mother had fallen pregnant to a man she didn't love. If she'd loved him she'd have stayed. She'd have fought. Kent women were fighters after all. No, Claudia must have had to make a choice, probably on her own, and she'd *chosen* to sacrifice her career at its pinnacle. To keep Nadia.

Nadia didn't even realise she was halfway back across the lobby until the woman on Reception called out her name. But she wasn't stopping for anything. Because Nadia wasn't in the same unimaginable position as her mother at all.

She didn't *have* to make a choice.

She *wanted* to.

And what she wanted was Ryder.

Sky High had been her saviour. The place she'd found her feet, found freedom. But that was then. Before she'd grown up. Before she'd gone home. And now she'd take her cramped little apartment, crazy-making Tiny Tots, the occasional ass-grab from salsa-dancing widowers, even occasional mind-bending conversations with her misfortunate mother if it meant she had *him*.

Eyes darting across the way, she spotted an empty cab

and leapt right on in, only to find it was the same one she'd just left.

The taxi driver looked up, surprised to find himself actually surprised. "Forget something, missy?"

Nadia shook her head, adrenalin pouring through her at such pace she could barely sit still. "Remembered something, actually. The airport, please."

"Well, then," he said, revving the engine and turning the cab into the arc of the driveway that took them back to The Strip, "ten minutes in Vegas and you're all done with the place. That's an honest to goodness first for me."

And even while Nadia's heart fair thundered against her ribs, the space that had been pressing so hard since the moment she'd left Australian shores no longer hurt. It settled, warmed…

And waited.

Ryder squinted against the sharp sunlight filtering through the clouds above. The car at his back quiet, its engine cool, its doors unlocked, its presence forgotten.

The large brown building before him sunned itself in the morning's warmth like an old alley cat—worn, neglected, clearly in its twilight years. And yet Ryder's gaze was fixated higher—on the row of arched windows reflecting the sun like mirrors on the top floor.

And he silently cursed his sister.

A week earlier he'd handed over all the work on his desk to his shocked employees and left the office. Then, he had boarded the first plane to Vegas, intending to knock on each and every one of the million hotel-room doors in the big, vibrant, elusive city, until he found Nadia.

Sam, still honeymooning, had met him at the airport and looked at him as if he'd gone off the rails. She'd turned out to be right.

Sam had looked up on Google the casino in which Sky

High would be performing later in the year. He'd called. No Nadia Kent was booked in. And hell if he knew her grandmother's name, the name she'd once told him she'd danced under. Meaning she could be anywhere, no doubt becoming more and more ensconced within that dazzling, decadent place with every second that passed.

So he'd gone home, only to end up back to the building housing the Amelia Brandt Dance Academy so often it was practically a second home. All to no avail.

Now he'd reached the end of his patience. If it took for him to stage a sit-in in order for Amelia Brandt herself to tell him where Nadia was, then that was what he'd do.

Then a flutter of movement appeared at the window. A flicker of dark hair, a press of a pale hand. It was doubtless all in his head, some desperate manifestation of his desire, but he was through the cracked front doors and up the rickety stairs before he even knew he was moving.

It was too late before he remembered that at some point on Tuesdays the studio took seniors pole-dancing—and that he might be about to witness something no man in his prime ever should—because he'd already pushed through the studio doors.

Music filled his ears. Music and giggles and the sound of a hundred elephants thundering across the floor. But the daylight pouring through the windows had hit him right in the eyes. A hand as a shield, he blinked away the spots, and then promptly forgot how to breathe.

For there she was, chatting and laughing with a tall lean woman in black while a bunch of little girls in ridiculous pink tutus went mad in the background.

Nadia.

He was sure he hadn't said her name, that his thought had been enough to capture her attention. As her ever-dancing hands stilled, her pointing toes lay flat against the floor. And she turned.

Ryder might as well have been slammed across the head with a plank as in the next moment his life flashed before his eyes. Only it wasn't his past. Not his father, or Sam, or the business that had taken him so far off course from his original dream as to make it unrecognisable.

It's you, Ryder thought, his future hovering in front of him like a juicy red apple just waiting to be plucked. *You're it. You're the one who makes my heart race and my bed warm and I'll take that for ever thank you very much.*

And when she began to walk his way, he felt the same way he had the first time, stunned by the instant impact of her earthy beauty, the awareness that sprinted up and down his arms, the eyes that looked past the all the nonsense and consequential career and fancy wheels and right into his soul. A place he'd avoided for a very long time, a place he'd rediscovered because of her.

"Ryder," she said, licking her lips as if his name were as sweet as honey. "I was just about to come and find you. Bearing gifts."

At which point she glanced beside him. He followed her gaze to the pink velvet chaise longue, where beside her patchwork handbag sat a massive net bag filled with apples.

He coughed out a laugh, surprise and desire gathering within him like a perfect storm. When he turned back to her, his smile had a dangerous edge. There was only one gift he'd take from her, and it didn't come in a bag.

It started with a touch. Although worried about for ever damaging the psyches of a plethora of sparkly, pink three-year-olds, Ryder held out a hand. Nadia took it. When he ran his thumb down the centre of her palm and she sighed, desire morphed into need. Need to have, to know, to *keep.*

"You're back," he said, his voice barely a hum.

She nodded.

"For good this time?"

"Depends."

"On?"

"Well, I quit my job when I left, and then I quit my *next* job to come back here. And then the airline went and lost my luggage. So I am currently homeless and unemployed and without stuff. If there's a way I can get those things sorted, then I'm home free."

Feeling as if the pieces of his life were floating about his head, just waiting to settle into perfect place, Ryder said, "I may have the solution."

"Really?"

"I always keep a spare toothbrush on hand, and you already look better in my shirts than I do."

Nadia let out a breath and Ryder wondered how long she'd been holding it. Unable to hold back any more, he pulled her closer, close enough to see the sparks of hope and swirls of shifting desire in her dark eyes.

He spared a glance over her shoulder where a dance teacher—possibly even Amelia Brandt herself—was watching with one hand to her heart and another to her cheek.

"She's the best dancer you'll ever see, and you know it. Give her a job!" he barked.

The dance teacher jumped, nodded, and proceeded to herd the tutu brigade into some sort of line away from the big grumpy man.

But Ryder needed more privacy than that in order to do what he intended to do. He grabbed Nadia's gear and tugged her out the door. Noise spilled from the floor below for the first time since he'd ever set foot in the joint, as what seemed like a never-ending stream of uni-student types in too-skinny jeans and ironically labelled T-shirts bundled into the dubious writers' centre space on the second floor.

When it looked as if the procession would never end, Ryder took the only option. He pulled open the doors of the lift, which now swung happily at the top floor. And as he wrenched the old glass doors closed, then the rusty wrought iron bars behind them, the sounds of the stairwell lowered to a mere hum.

"Daring," Nadia said, looking up through the glass ceiling to the old cables hulking above, before jumping up and down till the thing began to swing. "My kind of place."

The moment her eyes dropped back to his, hot, hooded, and dark with desire, Ryder dropped her bag and his apples, dragged her into his arms and kissed her as if his life depended on it. Hell, it did depend on it. And by the way she kissed him back—clinging, desperate, pressing herself into every part of him—her life *had* to depend on it too.

When he pulled away the ground beneath his feet continued to shift, even as the lift settled to a halt. He tipped his forehead against hers, waiting until their laboured breaths found a matching rhythm, and then he looked inside himself for the words he'd spent days trying to shape into some kind of sense.

"I'd like to give it a shot."

"What's that?"

"Adoring you."

At that she shuddered, her body melting against him, her head lying against his heart. Then she melted some more.

Intending to keep her there as long as he could, for ever sounded about right, Ryder ran his hand down her back, sliding his fingertips under the belt-line at her waist, her warm skin sending his heart rate thundering and turning his vision red. He kept it together, just, because there was more he intended to say. More she deserved to hear.

"I've been thinking for some time now that it's a damn shame a woman like you hasn't felt adored. And I want to be given the chance to be the man who adores you on a regular basis. Daily. Multiple times a day. Every minute. Every second."

He pulled back to find Nadia's head still tipped down. Her eyes closed. And when he propped a finger beneath her chin and tilted her face to his, he saw tears flowing down her cheeks. He leant in and kissed them away.

"Ryder," she said on a gulp.

"Yes, Nadia."

"I love you."

Well, he thought, his face splitting into a smile, *I should have just started with that*. "I know, sweetheart. This I do know. What I need to know, for sure, is if you're sure about being back. I know how much getting that job meant to you—"

She shut him up with a finger to his lips, and it took everything not to suck it into his mouth and taste her. Every bit of her. By the darkness that spilled into her eyes he knew she was feeling it too.

Rather than tempt fate, she curled her finger away and lay her hand on his chest, right over the beating of his heart. "I got all the way there, right up to the reception desk, but I couldn't check in. I couldn't pretend, even for a second, it was where I was really meant to be. Easiest decision of my life was to come back. To find you, Ryder. To tell you—"

"I love you too, Nadia," Ryder said.

It was Nadia's turn to beam, her smile turning her dark eyes bright, the utter happiness lighting that beautiful face sapping his breath straight from his lungs.

And in that moment, Ryder Fitzgerald—long-time lost thing—found himself.

All because he'd found her.

And now he was never letting her go.

This time the kiss was slow, this time deep, this time he took his time to bring her to the edge of thought and feeling. Because for the first time since he'd met her all they had was time. Years. For ever.

And then the lift began to move.

Nadia squealed, or at least Ryder hoped it had been her squeak that echoed in the small box.

"It works!" she said, laughing and spinning by that stage. "Near a year I've been teaching here and it's never worked."

"It's a sign."

"That while maintenance ignored Amelia's pleas they responded to her lawyers?"

"That this big slumberous lump of a building wants us here. Together. On one condition," said Ryder, waggling a finger at the lift as it drifted and screeched all the way to the ground floor. "No more dance lessons. Ever."

"Deal," said Nadia, sliding her hands around his waist as he pulled her deep into the circle of his arms, where she plastered herself against him, resting her cheek against his chest, her hip bumping his as the lift shook them side to side. "We can sway though. We're good at that."

"Yeah," he said, his voice a rumble, "we sway just fine."

They hit the ground with a thud and Ryder dragged the doors open, leaving them to spill into the sunshine.

Out on the street Nadia spread her arms, bags dangling from each hand, and closed her eyes and filled her lungs. With feet that seemed to float across the ground she twirled out into the middle of the deserted back street. "It feels like a brand-new day. Doesn't it?"

"A brand-new world," he agreed.

She looked over his car at him with a dark smile, a smile that spoke of cool sheets and hot limbs and getting all that as soon as possible, and said, "I do have a couple of hours before senior pole-dancing starts."

He laughed so loud it echoed off the buildings around them. "You little con-artist. You do have a job."

A shrug. Then, "For now. Until I find my real thing. Which I will do."

Ryder took her scarf and looped it around her neck, tugging her closer. "Of that I have no doubt. And...until then?" he asked, in a voice loud enough only she could hear it.

A finger running down the spine of his car, she sauntered around the thing, every step an exquisite sensuous thing he'd never become immune to. Neither did he want to. "I don't know—we could walk? Window-shop? Coffee?"

"I thought you hated coffee."

"Please, when did I say that?"

"First time I asked you out. *Stunts your growth* were your exact words. Miss Nadia, were you playing hard to get?"

"Ha! I've never played hard to get in my life. You just… overwhelmed me."

Ryder found it hard to imagine that this creature of his was overwhelmed by much in life, but he'd take it. "And now?"

"You still overwhelm me." At his side now, Nadia lifted onto her toes and pressed a soft, sweet kiss on his lips. Then, holding his cheeks between her palms, said, "Lucky for you I appreciate the thrill of being up high looking down, on stage looking out, eyes closed or blinded by stage lights, nothing but a ribbon and practice between me and certain death. But you, gorgeous man, are the greatest thrill of my life."

When she kissed him it was anything but sweet. It was deep, real, so far beyond a mere thrill.

"I'm thinking takeaway," said Ryder. "And they rent rooms above the pub around the corner, right?"

"Man after my own heart."

He held out an elbow, she slid her hand through the bend and rested her head on his big shoulder as together they walked down the thin Richmond street, sunlight filtering gently through the patchy clouds, the soft swish of their shoes on the crooked pavement in perfect time.

EPILOGUE

NADIA DODGED THE piles of plasterboard and plastic sails hanging from the scaffolding as she headed out of the soft double doors and down the stairs of the old Richmond building she now called home.

From the second-floor landing she caught Amelia's eye through the open doorway of the makeshift studio she was using while Ryder's company decked out the new slick arts studio near his old place in Brighton.

Wrangling a group of teenagers, no doubt forced to attend class to get ready for the senior formal, Amelia beckoned Nadia inside mouthing, *Help me!* But Nadia waved the appeal away. Been there, done that.

She wrapped her thick scarf around her neck and tugged her beanie tight about her ears, then pushed open the brand-new, shiny red doors at the front of the building and jogged down the tidy steps. Once she hit the far edge of the footpath, she walked backwards and as always marvelled at how warm her building looked even in the winter light with the scrubbed façade, windows all now free of bars and gleaming with the light of endeavour, the neat row of apple trees and box hedges planted along the entire front.

Hands in pockets and shoulders lifted high to her ears with pride, she glanced up at the arched windows of the third floor; the one with the window seat at which she sat and sketched ideas of a weekend. The other up against which their huge king-size bed had been shoved that first night the place was officially theirs and had never been moved. The next one that gave the most light for Ryder's vintage drafting table that he used in the morning while she slept in, the one that had been his mother's before him.

To think in a few short months it would all be done. The bottom floor for Ryder's new boutique firm—RF Renovations. The middle floor for her very own private studio—or her "swaying and swinging room" as Ryder called it. The top floor with its windows and beams, big industrial fans, crazy chandeliers and Ryder's imaginings for the layout of their first home, just gorgeous and perfect.

To think how much had changed since she'd made the choice to come home. After Vegas, she'd also made the choice to give her mother a break, because, no matter how tough the woman was, she mattered and always would. They were stuck with each other. Nadia had sat her mother down and told her exactly that and then had neatly put the onus on her mum to deal with it. Or not. Amazingly, she had. Slowly though. Kent women were stubborn after all.

"Hey, kiddo."

Nadia spun on her heels to find Ryder coming up the street towards her with breakfast for the crew: a tray of coffee and a bag of bagels from the most *amazing* pub just around the corner. It had become their local. For coffee, and for occasional accommodations when they couldn't wait for the restoration crew and/or dance students to vamoose for the night.

"Hey, handsome!"

Ryder's beautiful face broke into a grin. She'd thought the man the most gorgeous male specimen on the planet in his slick suits and shiny shoes. Turned out in old jeans, long-sleeved T-shirt and plaster dust in his hair he was even better.

"Off to work?" he asked, leaning in for a kiss.

"And lucky I'm not late. You were meant to wake me," she chastised.

"You looked too rumpled to move. I like you rumpled."

Coming over all warm, she hooked a finger into the beltline of his jeans and tugged. "Rumpled will not endear me to my new boss."

Ryder scoffed. "Your new boss adores you. The crazy, high-flying, death-defying acrobats you are choreographing adore you. I adore you. Now shut up and give me a kiss and get out of here. Or you'll really be late."

Nadia did as she was told, wrapping herself around her man while he held coffee and bagels out of her way.

"Here." He gave her a coffee and she gave him one last kiss. "Go teach them a thing or two."

"Planning on it," Nadia threw over her shoulder.

"If they need to know how to sway—"

"I know who to ask!" she added with a laugh.

And even as the laughter faded, the smile stayed. Stuck. A permanent fixture. Like so much else in her life. Her extraordinary, adorable life.

* * * * *

A sneaky peek at next month...

MODERN tempted™

FRESH, CONTEMPORARY ROMANCES TO TEMPT ALL LOVERS OF GREAT STORIES

My wish list for next month's titles...

In stores from 17th January 2014:

- ❑ No Time Like Mardi Gras – Kimberly Lang
- ❑ The Last Guy She Should Call – Joss Wood

In stores from 7th February 2014:

- ❑ Romance For Cynics – Nicola Marsh
- ❑ Trouble On Her Doorstep – Nina Harrington

Available at WHSmith, Tesco, Asda, Eason, Amazon and Apple

Just can't wait?

Visit us Online

You can buy our books online a month before they hit the shops! **www.millsandboon.co.uk**

0114/31

Special Offers

Every month we put together collections and longer reads written by your favourite authors.

Here are some of next month's highlights—and don't miss our fabulous discount online!

On sale 7th February

On sale 17th January

On sale 7th February

Find out more at
www.millsandboon.co.uk/specialreleases

Visit us Online

0214/ST/MB456